FALLING FOR THE FORWARD

A FAKE MARRIAGE HOCKEY ROMANCE

LOVE ON THE LINE
BOOK ONE

BRENDA ROTHERT

CHAPTER ONE

Suki

I OPEN MY APARTMENT DOOR, groaning when I see a massive box addressed to "Naughty by Nature" sitting on the ground. After closing the door, I sigh and hang my head, pinching the bridge of my nose.

"More dildos?" my best friend Mara asks absently from the couch.

I sigh heavily and press my back to the door. "I just wanted a relaxing day off. I need to do laundry and I wanted to catch up on *Survivor*. Now we have to haul another superheavy box to the storage place and I'll be thinking about how much I hate Tyler the entire time."

"You do have impeccably bad taste in men." She

closes the law textbook she's reading and takes off her glasses. "Let's just get it done. We can pick up Starbies on the way home."

I nod, knowing not even a vanilla bean Frap with extra caramel and whipped cream will lessen my urge to hunt down my ex-boyfriend. He left the country almost three months ago, ditching not only me but also his debts. That means I--the naive girl-friend who cosigned on a massive loan for his new adult toy business--lost my life savings and now have creditors after me.

Mara helps me drag the box into the apartment. When she pulls a box cutter out of her pocket, I pinch my brows together in a disgruntled look.

"Why waste time opening it? We know it's yet another one of Tyler's obnoxious organic sex toys that I'll spend the rest of my life paying for."

She shrugs. "We're going to have to sell this stuff at some point to help get you out of debt. We need to know what we've got."

I flop onto my favorite worn-out recliner, waiting for Mara's one-woman comedy routine to start. She's been my greatest ally since I split with Tyler, but sometimes I'm not in the mood to laugh about Naughty by Nature. Today is one of those days.

"Holy hell, that's a lot of butt plugs!" She reaches into the box and pulls out a large neon-green plug.

"The Alien Invader," I murmur. "The company told Tyler the materials were on back order and it would take a long time to fulfill it."

She bursts out laughing. "The Alien Invader? I don't care what it's made of, no one wants their bunghole *invaded*."

"I told him that."

She's still laughing. Mara even does the little snort thing she always does when she's laughing so hard she's about to pee.

"Did he seriously think people care whether their dildos and butt plus are nontoxic and BPA-free? It's not something I've ever cared about."

I don't respond because we've had this conversation several times. I thought Tyler's Stanford business degree meant he had good business sense. He sold me on his all-natural adult toy business over dinner at a tapas place one night, telling me it had the potential to make us seven figures a year within five years.

Us. That was what really did me in. I'm twenty-six, and when my boyfriend of more than three years started mentioning *us* and *the future*, I got heart eyes and lost all sense of reason.

What a fool I was. I can't even bring myself to tell

anyone but Mara about the financial grave I dug for myself. Not even my family knows. I'm working two jobs to keep up with the loan payments and not starve, and even though I'm broke as hell, I'll keep doing it as long as I have to.

Anything to spare me the humiliation of admitting I didn't just get dumped by a man I thought was in love with me. But I'm also going to be paying off his debts for the next twenty years while he's probably wining and dining his next victim.

————————

"So you're still liking the new job?" Mara asks on the drive home from my rented storage bay, where we dumped off the box of Alien Invaders.

"I love it. The girls keep me so busy that ten hours a day feels like about three. And they've gotten used to me, I think." I'm in my third week as a nanny for Carter Stanton, a pro hockey player for the Cleveland Crush. When I signed up at the nanny agency a month ago because I hated my boring office job, I never imagined I'd be hired the next week to take care of three little girls who lost their mother unexpectedly last month.

"Has your boss gotten any friendlier?"

I laugh because "friendly" isn't a word I'd ever use

to describe Carter. He's gruff, relaying the essential information I'll need every day before leaving for practice or a game with barely even a goodbye to the girls.

"No, but I don't see much of him. I just leave when he gets home, like I do when the weekend nanny gets there."

I usually waitress at a local sports bar on the weekends, but the bar is closed for the owner's vacation, so I have a rare weekend off.

Mara scowls. "Those poor kids. Their mom died and they got shipped across the country to live with an uncle who brings in strangers to take care of them."

I shrug. "He can't help his work schedule. And the agency vets nannies thoroughly. I had to have five references and a background check."

"I looked him up online. He's hot, but he seems like an asshole."

I park my old sedan in our designated spot in our building's parking lot. "You can't tell whether someone's an asshole by looking at their picture."

Mara scoffs. "I do it on Tinder every day and I haven't been wrong yet. Also, I'm not just basing it on his picture. I read articles. A reporter saw him smashing a hockey stick in the locker room after a game because he was so pissed about his team losing. It was probably roid rage."

I shake my head. We've been friends since high school, and Mara has always been quick to judge and slow to change her mind. I should be used to it by now.

"I think they test for that."

"Guess he's just an asshole then," she says. "You should definitely accidentally walk into his bathroom when he's getting out of the shower sometime and see if he's hung. All the guys with great dicks are assholes. It's so unfair."

We both get out of the car, meeting up behind it to walk into the building.

"I'll pass because, first of all, that's a disgusting thing to do, and also, it's a great way to get fired. I can't keep my alcoholic best friend supplied with wine if I lose my job."

"I prefer *wine enthusiast* to *alcoholic*."

"Are you studying today?"

She groans as she takes out her key to unlock our door. "Yeah, unfortunately. I'm over studying for the bar every waking minute. I just want to rot and drink."

I can't wait for Mara to take the bar exam in a couple of weeks so she'll stop stressing about failing it. We've been roommates since we both graduated from Ohio State four years ago. I planned to use my marketing degree for the business Tyler and I started, but it's been such a catastrophic failure that I can't even think about another marketing job. I've always loved kids and I now wish I would have gotten a teaching degree instead. So far, nannying doesn't even feel like work. Olivia, Charlotte and Hallie are sweet girls who are still grieving the loss of their mom and adjusting to their new lives. Getting to help them with those things is more gratifying than any job I've ever had.

I didn't realize how much I needed a fresh start. When I'm with the girls, I don't feel like a loser who got duped by a con man. We talk and laugh. I still think about them on the weekends and I'm always thrilled to see them again on Mondays.

Once we're back in the apartment, I walk into the kitchen and grab a can of pizza Pringles, grabbing a stack and then passing the can to Mara as she sits down on the couch. "Are Dex and Harry doing trivia tonight? I might actually be able to go if I get my laundry done."

SHE LIGHTS UP. "I'll text Dex. I deserve beer and bar nachos for dinner."

"I'm on a ramen budget, but I'm definitely down for trivia."

"We're eating at the bar, and I'm buying. You deserve dinner out after that shipment of The Asshole's Alien Invaders."

I remember being skeptical of Tyler's idea for a butt plug that had the word *invader* in the name, but as usual, I acquiesced. *Trust me, babe,* he said.

"How could I have been so stupid?" I ask for at least the hundredth time since he ghosted me.

"Good dick blinds us all, sweetie."

I sigh softly. "It was marginal dick."

Mara points at me and practically yells. "Finally, you're admitting it! I *knew* it! You said he was good in bed, but you never looked satisfied after a night with him."

"I'm in no mood for your shit," I warn.

"Bet I know what you *are* in the mood for since you haven't had decent sex in like four years."

"I will stab you in the eye. You'll be a pirate attorney with an eye patch."

"Yo-ho! I'd rock the shit out of an eye patch."

I laugh at her enthusiasm. My favorite thing about Mara is her relentless determination to be *Mara*. She always--one hundred percent of the time--has an opinion to offer and a joke to make. Our friends Harry and Dex say they plan to come to court once she works her way into the courtroom. Just to be entertained by watching her have to stay quiet.

I'm not like Mara. I don't have many crisply defined personality traits. Maybe...punctuality? But that's not exactly something people flock to. I'm mostly easygoing, not *un*attractive, and I'm a pretty good cook. Overall, I'm more forgettable than I'd like to be.

"My phone's in my bag. Can I use yours to text Dex?" Mara asks.

I pass it to her.

"Looks like you got texts from Dex and Carter."

"Carter?" I take the phone back.

Carter: Hi Suki, it's Olivia, I borrowed Uncle Carter's phone to text you. Sorry to bother you on your day off but Hallie really wanted me to show you this picture she drew.

I enlarge the attached photo, which is a crayon drawing of a smiling monster with seven arms and rainbow polka dots. Six-year-old Hallie loves to draw--it's one of our favorite after-school activities. I text back.

Suki: Hi Olivia! You are never bothering me, I'm so happy you sent this. Please tell Hallie this is very creative and I love her use of color.

I read the text from Dex next.

Dex: Trivia tonight? Mara said you're off and we need

you two in case there are questions about random TV shows or Taylor Swift songs.

Suki: And here I thought you wanted to see us....

Dex: Well, that too...I want to hear all about the hockey hottie you're working for.

Suki: He's straight and grouchy.

Dex: Rawr. I don't want him for me, I want him for you. He's grouchy and commanding, I hope?

Suki: It's not happening. I just work for him.

Dex: I recommend you drop something while standing in front of him, then drop to your knees and look up at him while biting your lip. Maybe refer to him as 'sir'...

Suki: I'm not attracted to him and I can't lose my job. We'll see you tonight.

Dex: He's going to put his puck in your net at some point. I know it, and I love that for you.

Suki: I'm never dating again. Go brush up on questions about presidents, you guys choked last time and that's your category.

Dex: On it. See you soon, dollface.

CHAPTER TWO

Carter

I STAND up from my seat on my closed toilet, flushing it for good measure. The only break I get from Hallie and Charlotte's nonstop questions is when I'm showering or sitting on the can. Do I come in here even when I don't have to go? Yeah, so I can have a little bit of peace.

"There you are!" Hallie runs up to me as soon as I walk downstairs. "Uncle Carter, you poop a lot."

"I eat lots of fiber."

"What's fiber?"

"It's something healthy foods have."

She grins, her toothy smile and brown curls

reminding me of my sister when she was a kid. "I want some fiber. Can we have it for dinner?"

"I'll see what I can do."

I order from DoorDash every night I'm home because I can't cook. Suki has been cooking on the days she's here, and she's a damn good cook. Today's a Sunday off for me, so the girls had some of Suki's homemade granola bars for breakfast and I made them grilled cheese for lunch, which is about the extent of what I can handle cooking. We'll order in for dinner.

"Will you color with me?" Hallie asks.

I sigh inwardly. I've already colored for more than two hours today. It's hard to say no when she gives me those big, hopeful eyes, though.

"Sure. What are your sisters up to?"

She takes my hand and walks me into the kitchen. "Olivia's watching a show with kissing and Charlotte's doing her hair."

Sounds innocent enough. Hallie sits down and I take the chair across from hers at the small table on one side of my kitchen.

It's a damn good thing I bought a huge house when I got traded to Cleveland four years ago. I chose it so I could be in a secure, gated community after one of my old teammates had a crazed fan show up at his house with weapons after a game loss.

The house sat mostly empty until five weeks ago when I got a phone call telling me Rachel had passed away in her sleep from an undiagnosed heart condition at age thirty-six. She was only five years older than I am now. My aunt Rosie met me in San Diego, where we buried my sister, packed up three grieving little girls and came back here.

Aunt Rosie stayed for a week to help the girls get settled. She's been like a second mom since my mom--her sister--died nine years ago. But unfortunately, she's a busy tech exec in Silicon Valley who never had kids and couldn't take on the responsibility of helping me any longer.

I'll never know why Rachel left her daughters to me in her will. Surely she had friends who would've been better than me at this.

"What are you drawing, Uncle Carter?" Hallie asks me.

"This is more manifesting. It's me holding up the championship cup at the end of the season."

"That's a big cup."

"Yep. What are you drawing?"

"Mommy in heaven."

Her small voice saying those words guts me. Rachel was a great mom and it's so fucking unfair she won't get to finish raising her daughters. I have perfunctory *uncle holding his baby niece* photos for each of them, but I never spent much time with them since we lived so far apart.

At least, that's one of the excuses I gave myself every time I declined an invite to fly to San Diego for holidays or just to visit and spend time hanging out with my nieces.

It's too far to travel. I'm too busy with hockey. I have to stay focused on my training to remain on top.

And now it's too late. My sister will never call me again and try to sweet-talk me into coming for Thanksgiving with promises of making Mom's oyster stuffing and pecan pie cheesecake. I'd give anything to get a call from her right now.

"Who's that?" I ask Hallie, who's drawing something small and brown next to the figure of Rachel with angel wings.

"A dog. Mommy and Charlotte are allergic to dogs, so we couldn't have one, but Suki said there are no allergies in heaven, so I think Mommy plays with dogs all the time."

This is fucking brutal. All three girls are trying to process the loss of Rachel, and not only am I hurting along with them, but I never know what to say. Even the nannies are better at comforting them than I am.

"I bet she is."

"I'm going to draw her twenty dogs. Do you think that's enough?"

"Yeah, I think petting twenty dogs would be enough to keep anyone pretty busy."

I look up when I hear someone walk into the room and see ten-year-old Charlotte. Her hair makes me do a double take. Earlier, her light-brown hair hung halfway down her back and now it's…gone.

"What the hell did you do?" The words fly out of my mouth as I take in the hatchet job on her hair. It's cut jagged and uneven at the nape of her neck and her bangs are short, half-inch-long spikes.

She gives me an unbothered look. "I cut my hair."

"I see that." I stand up and walk over to her. "Did it go the way you wanted?"

She shrugs, walks over to the fridge and takes out a bottle of apple juice. "I didn't want bangs anymore."

I'm supposed to have an argument for that. Rachel would. But it seems logical to me. She didn't want bangs so she cut off her bangs. And now she's going to get teased by asshole kids at school over it. Hell, the school might even think this is somehow my fault. That's the last thing I need as I'm trying to expedite the adoption process.

"Have you looked in a mirror?" I demand.

"Charlotte, no!" I've never seen the oldest of the girls, twelve-year-old Olivia, react so forcefully to anything. "What did you do?"

Olivia's eyes fill with tears as she walks into the kitchen and sees her sister's hair.

"Don't be so dramatic," Charlotte says with an edge.

"You look so bad!"

"Not as bad as you." Charlotte wrinkles her face in a sneer.

"Mom said we should never cut our own hair. You *ruined* it!"

I put a hand up. "Okay, girls. Let's not fight about it. It's already done."

"Give me the scissors," Olivia says sharply. "You don't get to have them anymore."

Charlotte slams her juice down on the kitchen island, liquid sloshing out of the bottle. "Stop trying to act like Mom!"

Olivia narrows her eyes and gives me a look. "Aren't you going to do something?"

"Like what? I can't put her hair back."

She pinches her brows together in an expression that reminds me so much of my sister I feel a tug in my chest. "You can't just do nothing! Take away the scissors! Punish her!"

Charlotte's hands are fisted at her sides. "It's not

your business, Olivia! You're the one who should be punished for watching an R-rated movie!"

Olivia's cheeks turn pink. I give her my best stern look. "You were watching an R-rated movie?"

"You're such a brat!" she yells at Charlotte.

"Me? I w--"

"That's it, girls!" I look between them. "Not another word out of either one of you."

Charlotte locks eyes with me, glowering. Olivia's gaze is fixed on the floor, her arms crossed. But they both stay quiet.

"Charlotte, you need to bring me every pair of scissors you have. From now on, you need to ask me before you use them."

Her mouth forms an indignant O. "What? That's not fair."

"I'm the law in this house, so I decide what's fair."

That's what my dad used to say when Rachel and I were kids. I hated it then, but it makes a lot of sense when you're standing on this side of an argument with a child.

I look at Olivia. "And you aren't allowed to watch anything on a screen without getting my permission first."

"Are you serious?"

"Very serious."

Charlotte starts to stomp off, but I say, "You need to clean up your mess."

She gets some paper towels and wipes up the juice, scowling. Olivia walks over to the fridge and opens it.

"What's for dinner?" she asks.

"I'll order something." I look at the clock and see that it's almost 4:30 p.m. "Do you guys want me to order now?"

"Can we get pizza?" Hallie asks, still coloring.

"We just had pizza last night," Charlotte says. "I want Chinese food."

"That's not healthy," Olivia says.

I grab a fresh piece of paper from the package of computer printer paper I bought for Hallie to color on. If only I could manifest peace between these girls. They can go from hugging to arguing in five seconds flat.

"What's your idea, then?" Charlotte demands of Olivia.

"We should eat something with vegetables."

"Chinese food has vegetables."

"Well, it's not healthy. We should eat something like Suki makes."

"I want cheesy soup," Hallie says to me.

One of the meals Suki made us last week was broccoli cheese soup, salad and bread, and it was great. All three girls had seconds. I wonder if I could convince Suki to come here and cook dinner on the weekends. With Chad, the girls' deadbeat dad, making rumblings about challenging me for custody of them, I need to do everything I can to make it clear in court that my home is more stable. Home-cooked meals can only help.

"I'll order from the Italian place," I say, settling it. "They have pizza, pasta, sandwiches, salads. Everyone can get whatever they want."

"Do they have Chinese food?" Charlotte asks.

Olivia rolls her eyes. "Of course not, you idiot. It's *Italian*."

"Don't call names." Hallie scolds Olivia from her seat at the table.

"Yeah." Charlotte gives Olivia a dirty look. "Don't call names."

"What are you going to do about her hair?" Olivia asks me.

I pretend to be focused on my drawing for a couple of seconds because I don't know what to say. But I have to sound like the authority figure. What the hell would Rachel do?

All three of them are looking at me expectantly. When I can't stall anymore, I say, "There's nothing I can do. She has to just grow it out."

Olivia balks. "You could get her a wig."

"I'm not wearing a wig!" Charlotte wails.

"At least it looks like normal hair."

I pick up my phone and get up from the table. I'm counting the minutes until I get to go to practice in the morning. The guys can put me in goal with no pads if they want and I'll happily take body shots. It would be better than mediating disputes between these bickering girls.

"Where are you going, Uncle Carter?" Hallie asks me.

I don't even look back as I say, "To the bathroom."

CHAPTER THREE

Suki

I'M REACHING out to ring Carter's doorbell for the third time in a row Monday morning when he whips the front door open, glowering.

"Um, hey," I say weakly, my brows hitting my hairline as I take him in.

He's only wearing a white towel wrapped around his waist, water glistening on his muscular chest like he just walked off the set of an ad for a manly body wash. His chest hair is just a tiny bit darker than his short brown hair, which is also dripping. And his abs are...not at all disappointing.

"Come on in," he says, stepping aside. "It's a shit

show in here. Olivia tried to cook breakfast while I was in the shower and it set off the smoke alarm."

My heart rate kicks up with concern. "Oh God, did something catch on fire?"

He shakes his head. "No, I think it was just smoke. But when Hallie yelled outside my bathroom door that the fire alarm was going off, I tracked water all over the floors running down here to make sure everyone was okay."

The proof is in the wet footprints on the wood stairs of the open stairway, continuing across the living room and into the open kitchen. There's still a cloud of smoke in the kitchen and from the smell of the air, it was bacon that Olivia burned.

"Olivia didn't wait for you to make breakfast," Hallie says to me in a tattletale tone.

I smile brightly. "Well, she tried to do something nice. And--" I fall silent when my gaze lands on Charlotte.

It looks like someone cut her beautiful chestnut hair with a dull knife. Her bangs are just a short row of spikes atop her forehead and the back is jagged. I turn to Carter, whose expression is neutral.

"Like I said, shit show. She cut her own hair yesterday."

"Where were you?" The accusatory question flies from my mouth.

He lowers his brows and grinds out, "I can't be in three places at once. I was coloring with Hallie."

I walk over to Charlotte and tuck her hair behind one ear, wanting to wrap her in a hug. A drastic haircut is a universal female cry for help, and poor Charlotte has to be hurting.

"Well, this is a look," I say, smoothing a hand over the top of her head.

She shrugs. "I like it."

I cup her cheeks in my hands. "Do you really? Because I can take you to a salon today to have this fixed."

Her eyes widen hopefully. "You can?"

"If your uncle is okay with you missing school today."

"That's not fair," Olivia gripes as she walks into the kitchen. "I have to go to school because I didn't chop off my own hair?"

Ignoring her jab, Charlotte and I both look at Carter, who shrugs. "I don't care." He gives Olivia a sharp look. "I'm going to finish my shower now. No more cooking. You guys can have cereal for breakfast."

"I'll make breakfast for them. Do you guys want French toast?"

It's one of the few things they all agree on every time I offer it.

Carter stalks back toward the stairway, and I can't resist a quick glance at his broad back. Which isn't just broad but also muscular. And maybe he's not *stalking*, but it sure seems that way because of his size and his mood.

I crack the kitchen windows to let in some fresh air and start gathering the ingredients for French toast. I always follow the recipe I learned from my mom, mixing up eggs, milk, flour, sugar, cinnamon and vanilla. Just the smell of the ingredients reminds me of my childhood.

Olivia is packing herself a lunch to take to school and Charlotte is organizing a folder of papers when Hallie blurts out, "I saw Uncle Carter's *butt*."

I turn to her, amused. She's covering her mouth with her hand and giggling.

"Gross, Hallie," Charlotte mutters.

Hallie continues in a loud whisper, undeterred. "There's hair on his butt."

"Ew." Olivia glares at her younger sister.

"Suki, do all boys have hair on their butts?" Hallie asks me.

I never thought I'd be discussing *that* with a six-year-old. "Some do. We're all made differently."

"Do girls have hair on their butts?"

"Hallie." Olivia gives her an exasperated glare. "Enough."

I set the first piece of dipped bread into a hot pan. "It's okay to be curious. Most women don't have hair on their butts, no."

"Do you?"

I pretend to peek in the back of my black leggings. "Nope."

Hallie is so sweet. It hurts my heart that she lost her mom so young. Of the three girls, Hallie is the one I can tell craves hugs and kisses the most, so I make sure to give her lots of hugs and I kiss the top of her head every time I drop her off at school and leave the house for the day.

"Nancy isn't as nice as you," Charlotte says a few minutes later, the four of us sitting around the table.

I had a protein shake at home, so I'm sipping coffee while they eat their French toast. "Who's Nancy?"

"She's the lady who comes over when you're busy," Hallie says.

"The weekend nanny," Olivia explains. "She was here Saturday."

"She's on her phone all the time and she makes gross food." Charlotte wrinkles her nose.

Carter walks into the kitchen, carrying a packed duffel bag and dressed in black shorts and a gray hoodie with his team name and logo on it. He pours coffee into a travel mug and then looks over at me.

"You've got the schedule for the week from the agency. I'll be back on Thursday."

Hallie gets up and runs over to hug him, pressing her cheek to his stomach. "Good luck, Uncle Carter. I hope you win."

He pats her on the head, looking uncomfortable. "We'll give it our best shot."

I don't get how anyone could do anything but melt into a puddle when Hallie looks at them with those big brown eyes. It's all I can do not to open my arms and offer her a hug myself.

Hallie lets go of him and he picks up his travel mug and his bag, slinging the bag over his shoulder so he can grab his car keys. "See you guys later."

And that's it--he walks out the door and closes it behind him. I hold back an urge to roll my eyes. Anyone with a heartbeat should be able to give a better goodbye than that to three grieving little girls. He didn't even make eye contact with them.

A quick glance at the clock reminds me I don't have time to lament Carter's lack of warmth right now. "Hey girls, we need to get going. One minute to finish up and get your dishes into the sink, okay?"

I send a quick text to Carter, reminding him to call Charlotte's school to have her excused for the day, making sure I include the phone number, which

I have on a list of emergency phone numbers for the girls on my phone.

Hopefully he can spare a minute from his busy day to do that.

This time, I do roll my eyes.

———

"IT'S SO COOL," Charlotte gushes later that day. "I love it."

She hasn't stopped smiling since we left my hair stylist Andi's salon. Andi came in on her day off when I texted her and gave Charlotte a pixie crop and light-pink color. Her bangs still look *unintentional*, but it's much better than before.

"You have the perfect face for that cut," I tell her as we walk to my car from the ice cream shop we just went to.

Carter gave me a credit card to use for all the girls' expenses, and today, I didn't just use it for Charlotte's hair. I also took her shopping for new clothes and shoes. She's a natural at thrifting, and I got to hear about some of her mom's great finds at secondhand stores. It's the most Charlotte has ever talked to me, and it feels like an all-around win.

"Time to pick up your sisters," I say as we get in the car. "Let's not mention the ice cream."

She gives me a conspiratorial smile. "I won't."

We pick up Hallie first, who spills all the first-grade tea. Apparently Stormi broke up with Aiden and Aiden immediately asked Stormi's best friend, Ella, to be his girlfriend and she said yes.

"Ella, no!" I cry in mock dismay. "Sisters before misters!"

"They aren't sisters," Hallie says.

I grin at her in the rearview mirror. "Sometimes girls call their girlfriends sisters."

"Do you like my hair?" Charlotte asks, turning around so Hallie can get a good look.

Hallie gasps. "I want pink hair!"

"Uncle Carter will say no."

I give Charlotte a nervous look. "Crap. Should I have asked him before I let you get pink hair?"

She shrugs and sits back in her seat. "Too late now."

I should probably break the news to him myself so Charlotte's happiness over her hair isn't ruined by his ire when he sees it.

When I pull up to Olivia's middle school, she's waiting for us. She sighs heavily as she gets into the back seat. "Suki, are you good at math?"

"Uh...I should be able to help if it's sixth-grade math. What are you working on?"

"Areas of shapes. I have to memorize formulas."

"I can definitely help with that."

"Charlotte, your hair!" Olivia squeals. "Let me see it!"

Charlotte turns around. "Suki's hairstylist, Andi, did it. Isn't it great?"

"It's pretty," Olivia agrees. "Much better than before."

I give Olivia a grateful smile in the rearview. "Girls, what would your mom think about Charlotte's pink hair?"

"She would laugh!" Hallie says gleefully.

"I think she'd like it, but she wouldn't have liked me cutting it," Charlotte says.

"Hey, at least it's not a tattoo," I say. "It'll grow back."

"But I want to keep it pink, even when it's long."

I'm not sure that'll fly with her uncle, but I don't mention it.

"What should we have for dinner tonight?" I ask them. "I have groceries for spaghetti or tacos."

Hallie and Olivia vote tacos and Charlotte votes spaghetti.

"Could we do spaghetti tomorrow night?" I ask her.

"Sure."

When we get home, all the girls head off to do

their own things. I know the silence won't last long, so I take the opportunity to text Carter.

Suki: Hey Carter, just wanted to show you what we did with Charlotte's hair. She's very happy with it and I think she looks great.

I exhale hard before sending him the text and one of the photos I took of Charlotte at the salon. I'm about to set my phone on the counter and start dinner when I see that he texted me back right away. That's probably not good.

Carter: OK.

I squint at my phone screen, reading his message again. *OK?* What the hell kind of response is that? I want to like the guy--really, I do--but he makes it hard. Just because his nieces are here because of an unexpected tragedy, that doesn't mean it's okay for him to show so little interest in them.

A pastel hair color deserves something more than *OK.* Ignoring my voice of reason, which is telling me to be quiet and not piss off my new boss, I fire back a quick response.

Suki: Hope you have an OK game tonight.

I set my phone back down on the counter, my pulse pounding. That wasn't smart. Should I try to unsend it?

It's probably too late. I turn my phone screen-side down and start gathering my ingredients for dinner. I'm not going to waste another moment thinking about Carter's feelings.

If he even has any. Carter very well may be one of those cavemen who only think about sports, food and sex. In which case, he won't even know that was an insult.

Problem most likely solved.

CHAPTER FOUR

Carter

"Horseshit!"

I stir and sit up, blinking to focus in the darkened interior of the plane. My teammate Leo, who woke me up, is carrying on about losing a hand of poker. I glare across the aisle at him.

"What's got your panties in a bunch?" he asks.

"You woke me up."

He shrugs. "We're landing soon anyway."

I pick up my phone and look at the screen. It's 4:36 a.m. With a deep exhale, I lean my head back against my seat rest, hoping I can go back to sleep. I'm not ready to start another long day yet.

Our team plane got grounded a week ago for

repairs, so we're sharing planes with other teams and flying commercial to get where we need to go. You'd think it would be quieter on team planes, but commercial jets don't have tables and chairs for guys to play poker and bitch about losing as loudly as they want. It's supposedly an upside that we can fly out anytime on private planes, but I'm not a fan of waiting until 1:00 a.m. for the Chicago team's plane to arrive in Tampa so we can take it to Vancouver.

"Shit," Bash says from the seat beside me. "My phone's almost dead. You got a charger I can borrow?"

Sebastian Stone is my closest friend on the team. Actually, he's my closest friend, period. Me, him and Leo are the first offensive line of our team.

"You need it right this second?" I ask, my eyes still closed.

"Yeah, my phone's almost dead."

Who needs their phone at this hour, anyway? If I argue, Bash will bicker with me until I end up giving it to him, so might as well save myself the trouble. I pick up my backpack and unzip it, sorting through stuff in search of my extra charger.

"Did you sleep much?" he asks.

"Not enough. I haven't had a decent night of sleep since Saturday night."

"Yeah, I couldn't get back to sleep after that fire

alarm at the hotel Monday night, either. What was your problem on Sunday night and Tuesday night?"

"Tuesday night was last night, and we went from the game to the airport to this plane, where I couldn't sleep because you snore so loud. Sunday night, Hallie had a nightmare so she got in bed with me. I thought she'd go back to sleep, but she wanted to talk."

"About what?"

It takes me a second to remember everything. "How they get the lead inside pencils, whether zombies are real, why we can't breathe on the moon and what's on the inside of boobs."

Bash laughs. "I fucking love that kid, man. Did you guys ever go back to sleep?"

"Eventually. But I woke up again when she kicked me in the back."

"I keep telling you to get those girls a pet. Hallie could snuggle up with the pet when she has a nightmare and you can sleep through the night."

"And I keep telling you that Charlotte is allergic to dogs and cats, just like Rachel."

"So get them something else. Like an iguana."

I pass him the charger. "You think Hallie can snuggle an iguana? That would probably just give her more nightmares."

"Okay, so what about a pig?"

"A pig?" I furrow my brow.

"Yeah, like one of those teacup pigs. They're tiny and cute as hell."

"I don't want a fucking pig in my house."

"They're pets. You can house-train them just like dogs. I've seen TikToks about it."

I scoff. "It has to be true then."

"I'm serious, dude. Pigs are actually very clean and they don't sweat. They make good pets."

I think about it for a few seconds. "I don't know, maybe. How big do they get?"

"The micro ones stay small, like a dog. Twenty pounds or less."

All three girls are going to grief counseling, and Charlotte's counselor did mention to me that a pet could help comfort them. I try to be comforting, but I'm not great at it. And the bottom line is that no matter how much my life changed on the day Rachel died, the girls' lives changed more.

They lost their mom. The only parent they've ever really known. Chad took off right after Hallie was born and he's never paid a dime of child support. I've always made sure Rachel and the girls are taken care of, but until now, that meant sending Rachel money every month.

She didn't want to take it at first, but when I reminded her that a mom without financial worries is a happier mom, she couldn't disagree with me. No one but me and Rachel knew I was the one paying for Olivia's sleepaway summer camps and Charlotte's private violin lessons, and no one ever will.

The grief counselor told me I'll make mistakes and that the girls' emotions may be volatile for a while as they mourn their mom. I can always tell when Olivia's been crying because her eyes are red and her cheeks are splotchy, but she tries hard to be strong for her sisters. I think even she, the sensible, practical oldest sister, would like a pet.

A pet will add another layer of stress to our household, but if it will make them happy, it's worth it. I can't be there for them physically as much as I want to because of my travel schedule, and a pet would be a constant comfort they could always rely on.

I take out my phone and search for pet pigs for sale, making sure Bash can't see my screen.

"I know you're looking at porn," he mumbles.

"Uh-huh."

"Hey, before you put your hand down your pants and start jerking off, I've got to know--what *is* on the inside of boobs?"

I shake my head, not even bothering to respond.

———

IT'S RAINING IN VANCOUVER. I went back to the hotel for a pregame nap, and I got soaked when I got in and out of my Uber back to the arena. I needed the sleep, though, and I feel a lot better.

I head to the locker room to change into dry clothes, arriving just in time for a meeting with our head coach, Noel Turner.

"We've seen it in film--these guys come out swinging," he says. "They're gonna try to set the pace right out of the gate so they can dictate the game."

I follow along as he goes over plays on his whiteboard, but my mind is on the voicemail I listened to on the Uber ride back to the area.

My family law attorney, Michelle Maroni, is widely known to be the best in the Cleveland area. When one of my teammates found out his wife was cheating on him, he hired Michelle before even telling his wife he wanted a divorce, just to be sure his wife wouldn't hire her first. When he got traded to Boston last season, he was able to take his kids with him, thanks to Michelle's work on his behalf.

Michelle gets right to the point, telling me to call her as soon as possible. I can't stop worrying that something big has come up in my bid to adopt the girls. Even though Rachel left me guardianship of them in her will, Michelle recommended I adopt them. That means the girls' deadbeat dad, Chad, had to be tracked down and agree to it.

I'm holding out hope he'll do the right thing. He hasn't tried to see his three daughters since he left when Hallie was nine months old. Five years without a single effort made. Needless to say, I hate that fucker.

"You got somewhere better to be, Stanton?" Coach barks when he catches me looking at the clock on the wall.

"No, Coach."

"You sure? I don't want to keep you from anything."

He's fired up for this game because we've lost our last four games to Vancouver. They're one of the toughest teams to beat on their home ice.

"I'm good, Coach."

"I'm glad to hear it. We need our first line to be dialed in."

"We are," Leo assures him. "We're ready, Coach."

Leo's the best kind of teammate. He always tries to deflect blame from others onto himself. Especially when it's me or Bash. If Coach is telling us we fucked up, Leo tries to shift at least some of the blame onto himself.

"Be back here in fifteen," Coach says, capping the

black marker he was writing on the whiteboard with.

The other guys head out of the meeting room to grab drinks or use the bathroom. I approach Coach Turner.

"Hey, Coach, I need to return a call from my attorney about the girls. She said it's important. I don't know if I'll even catch her when I call, but I wanted to let you know in case I'm not back in time."

"No problem. Do what you need to do."

He's an intense coach, but he's always telling us family comes first. When Rachel died, he told me to take as much time as I needed. I knew he meant it, too. But every time I saw that we'd lost when I was in San Diego, I felt guilty about being gone.

That's a thing we all experience in hockey--our team becomes family, too, and we want to be there for our families and our team families at the same time sometimes. In the wake of my sister's unexpected death, all I wanted to do was hit opponents. I fought my way through my first two games back.

Nothing feels worse than helplessness. Seeing Olivia, Charlotte and Hallie devastated over losing their mom was so much harder for me than grieving Rachel was. Aunt Rosie told me to hug them and just let them cry, to stop trying to keep them from being so sad.

It's damn hard, though. My nature is to hold things up as they're breaking. To keep them from falling and shattering. But the girls had already cracked into a thousand pieces. I still feel like I'm picking them up, which I'm not great at.

I take my phone into an empty training room, flip the light switch on, and push a button on my screen to call Michelle back.

"Hey, Carter," she says, answering her cell immediately. "Thanks for getting right back to me, I know how busy you are."

"No problem, what's up?"

"The response from Chad Sanderson's attorney was filed." I can hear the grimace in her tone. "I don't like the looks of it. He's living in Seward, Alaska, and he's been employed at the same place for more than two years. He's engaged to a woman and they're expecting a child. And he wants full custody."

I shift, tensing as I pace across the room. "He hasn't tried to see them in five years, though. And Rachel made me their guardian."

"He's their biological parent, though."

"Technically, but he's a piss-poor excuse for a father. Excuse my language."

"Don't worry about it. He's a deadbeat, to put it mildly. I reached out to his attorney--"

"So the guy who can't afford child support can

afford an attorney?" I shake my head and look at the ceiling. "I paid you twenty grand. Is that what he's paying?"

"I don't know, but...I get it. And you won't be surprised that his attorney inquired about whether Rachel had life insurance."

"Are you fucking kidding me?" I roar, not caring who can hear me. "He wants to make money when my sister's cold in the ground?"

"The attorney said he wants to know if there would be life insurance to provide for the children."

I'm so pissed I think my head might actually blow off my shoulders. "Yeah, like hell it would go to the girls. I'm not letting him take them to Alaska. They don't even know him. Rachel didn't want this."

She clears her throat. "I understand your frustration. Nothing has been decided yet. But here's my advice." I close my eyes and take a deep breath, forcing myself to dial it back and listen. "We need to establish that your home is the most stable place for the children. You said you had an aunt who helped you with the children after your sister passed away-- have her come for a visit for a few days. If you have a girlfriend you're considering proposing to at some point, move that up."

I balk at that. "A *wife*? What, like I can't do this alone because I'm a man?"

This throat clearing feels more assertive. "Mr. Stanton, who's caring for the children right now?"

"A nanny."

"When you're on the road, traveling overnight and on weekends, who's caring for the children?"

I see where she's going with this, and my aggravation flares. "Nannies. You want me to quit hockey? Is that what I'll have to do?"

"No. But we need to show that you have *family* helping, not paid nannies."

"My aunt Rosie is the only family I have left."

"Then get her there for a visit. And I also need to know, did your sister have life insurance to provide for the children?"

I sigh and run a hand through my hair. "Yeah, it was like two hundred and fifty thousand dollars. I was planning to divide it into three trusts for the girls."

The couple seconds of silence on the other end of the line tell me something I don't want to hear.

"Okay." I nod and take another deep breath. "I'll get Aunt Rosie to come for a visit and I'll...work on the other thing."

"I can hold off on filing a response for a couple weeks. I know it's not ideal since your career is so demanding, but--"

"No, it's--I've got it. This is the most important thing. I'll get it done."

"If it's not the right time to get married, I'm not saying it's a deal-breaker. But leaving the children with family when you have to travel for work as much as you do is always preferred by the court."

"I understand."

"Okay, keep in touch and we'll talk before I send a response."

I sit down on the training table. "Listen, if it comes down to me quitting hockey or losing the girls, I'll quit."

I didn't realize how strongly I felt about it until now when I found out I could lose the girls to Chad. I may not be a natural nurturer, but they'll always have a safe place with me, and I'll do anything it takes to protect them. Even if it's their own father I have to protect them from.

"We're going to do everything we can to avoid that," Michelle says.

"Okay."

"Let's do our best to show the court you have a stable home with help from other family. I win a lot more cases than I lose, so don't panic, okay?"

"Yeah. Okay."

We end our call and I stand up, reeling from the news about Chad being engaged and living in fucking Alaska. No wonder Rachel's private eyes couldn't find him to drag child support out of him.

I hardly have any family left, and I'll fight like hell with anyone who messes with what I do have.

There are only two things I want to do right now: punch Chad until he has no teeth left and talk to my sister.

Unfortunately, neither one is an option.

CHAPTER FIVE

Suki

"What's that glow under your covers?"

I know exactly what it is. Charlotte is supposed to be off her phone and in bed by nine thirty, but it's not the first time I've caught her on it when I snuck up to her door to check in on her around 10:00 p.m.

The glow quickly disappears. "It's nothing."

I step into her room, closing the door so I know the other girls can't hear me. I hate having to be stern with the girls, but sometimes it's necessary. "Hey, I don't lie to you. Please treat me with the same respect I treat you with."

There's a pause, and then, "I was on my phone. Sorry, Suki."

"I appreciate the honesty. If it happens again, I'm going to start taking your phone away every night at nine."

She sighs. "Okay."

"Night, Charlotte."

"Good night."

I leave her room, holding back a smile. Charlotte reminds me so much of my brother Nate. When my mom married my stepdad when I was three, my stepdad was a widowed father of three boys, and Nate's the middle one. He pushed our parents' boundaries as far as he could, but he was still a good kid.

I peek into Hallie's room and see she's curled up on her side with her arms wrapped around her favorite stuffed bear, George. I tiptoe in and cover her back up, then pull her door almost all the way closed. She likes me to leave it cracked with the hallway light on in case she wakes up and gets scared.

We had a quiet evening at home. I made beef stew and mashed potatoes for dinner and helped all three of them with homework, and then we watched *The Great British Baking Show*, our new before-bed ritual. We all get into Carter's king-size bed and snuggle up under the covers with popcorn.

Olivia seemed down tonight. So even though she's in bed with the lights out, I walk into her room to check on her. She seems to be sleeping soundly, and I'm about to turn around and leave the room when I see her shoulders shudder slightly.

"Olivia?" I rush to crouch beside her. "What's wrong?"

My heart races with fear that she's having a seizure, but then I see that she's crying. She sniffles and wipes her cheeks with her fingers.

"I'm fine."

I reach over to her bedside table and switch on the lamp. Her splotchy face is illuminated by the light's soft glow.

"You aren't fine. What's going on?" I stroke a hand over her head, smoothing her hair.

"Tomorrow's my birthday," she says softly.

My eyes fly open in alarm. Why the hell didn't Carter tell me? He was supposed to be home from his road trip by five this evening, but he texted me that his team was having plane issues and it would be more like eleven. I was planning to go sleep at home and come back in the morning, but if I'd known tomorrow was Olivia's birthday, I would have been planning for it today.

I have no gifts for her. No cake. I imagine myself

giving Carter the dick punch he deserves, but it doesn't make me feel any better.

I'll figure something out tomorrow. For now, I have to figure out why Olivia is so upset.

"Are you unhappy about your birthday?" I ask gently.

Fresh tears well in her eyes and she whispers, "I don't want a birthday without my mom."

It guts me. Seeing the girls mourn a mom who so obviously loved them more than anything is the hardest thing I've ever done.

"Did your mom make your birthdays special?"

"Yeah. She always sings us 'Happy Birthday' at the exact time we were born. I was born at 4:24 p.m."

When I feel like I don't know how to handle the grief the girls are going through, I ask myself what my mom would do. She always told me not to shove my feelings down. To *feel* them, good or bad.

I sit on the edge of Olivia's bed, turning to face her. "That had to be one of the happiest moments of her life. Meeting you for the first time."

She sniffles. "She was in labor for sixteen hours. She cried when she held me."

"I think your mom would still want you to have a birthday, even if she can't be here to celebrate it with you."

I can tell she's holding back tears as she responds. "I'll just think about her and cry."

I put a hand on her shoulder. "That's okay. My dad died when I was one. I don't remember him, but I still cry when I see pictures of him and think about him."

"Really?"

"My mom says sometimes tears are love overflowing out of you."

"I miss my mom."

"What would feel better for you? A birthday like you would have celebrated with your mom, or something different?"

She considers. "Something different."

"How about if you stay home from school tomorrow and we start your birthday with some chocolate chip waffles?"

She's quiet for so long I think she's going to say no, but finally, she says, "I like waffles."

"Then waffles it is." I don't usually hug and kiss Olivia, but something makes me lean down and kiss the top of her head. "And then we'll do whatever sounds fun to you."

I stand up and smooth a hand over the covers she has pulled up over her shoulders. I wish I had something wise and comforting to say, but I think I should let her feel sad. Hopefully I can make tomorrow into more than a day she just gets through.

"Good night," I say softly.

"Night, Suki."

I switch off the lamp and leave the room, closing the door behind me. When I get downstairs to the kitchen, I unload the dishwasher and wipe down the counters.

Though I know I should sit down and relax, I can't. I'm too angry at Carter. I don't know which will piss me off more--if he doesn't know tomorrow is Olivia's birthday or if he knows and forgot to tell me.

It's no wonder he doesn't have a girlfriend. He's too self-centered to think of anyone else's wants and needs. The guy probably looks at selfies when he jerks off.

I want to rant over this to Mara, but that'll just get me even more worked up. So, I organize the pantry instead. The pantry is bigger than my bathroom at my apartment, but Carter doesn't have anything sorted. He's clearly a bulk shopper; there are cases stacked on cases of Goldfish crackers, fruit snacks and juice boxes.

The mental image of Carter pushing a flatbed through Costco and loading it up with the girls' favorite snacks softens me slightly.

No, Suki. No softening. He deserves a swift fist to the dick. Full stop.

I lose track of time, and when he walks from the door connecting the garage to the kitchen a little after eleven, the kitchen table is filled with things I moved there so I can organize.

His brow furrows as he says, "Hey."

"Hi." My tone is crisp, but I'm proud of how little bite it has. I'm so restrained.

"How are the girls?"

"Good. Olivia's pretty upset about tomorrow, though."

The wrinkle between his brows deepens. "What's going on tomorrow?"

I narrow my eyes in an icy glare. "Her birthday."

His eyes widen and he takes a couple seconds to respond. "Fuck. Her birthday."

"You completely forgot?" I whisper-hiss, walking over to him with a *less-than-restrained* scowl. "You are *mind-blowingly* selfish. Like...how do you even do it?" I throw my hands in the air. "Do you practice this level of arrogance, or are you just gifted?"

His lips part with surprise as he returns my glare. "Do you usually talk to your bosses this way?"

"My *boss*." I roll my eyes and cross my arms. "Fire me if you want--it would be another staggeringly selfish move on your part. I never met Rachel, but I guarantee she'd be letting you have it right now if she were here."

He flinches and I feel a little guilty. I've spent the past hour getting angrier and angrier and I just unleashed a fire hose of fury on him. I sigh and pinch the bridge of my nose.

"Okay, you're right," I say softly. "That wasn't my place."

He puts a palm up, looking sheepish. "No, you're right. I should have put calendar reminders on my phone. I'll do that before I go to bed tonight."

I nod, a little lightheaded as it sinks in that I didn't just get myself fired from the job I desperately need.

"I told her she can miss school tomorrow and I'll make her favorite waffles and take her to do whatever sounds fun."

"Is she upset because she knows I forgot about it?"

My heart sinks as I remember finding Olivia crying. "No, she was very upset when I went to check on her at ten and that's why I found out tomorrow is her birthday. She said she doesn't want to have a birthday without her mom."

Emotions flood Carter's eyes and he looks away. It hits me that my assumptions about him were wrong. He's devastated--about his sister, the pain her oldest daughter is in, or both.

He clears his throat. "If you can give me two hours, I'll make an appearance at practice and then spend the day with her."

"I don't mind doing it. I'll make sure she has fun."

He nods. "I know you would. Honestly, Suki..." He still can't meet my eyes. "You're the best thing that has happened for the girls since Rachel died." He clears his throat again and I realize he's trying to keep himself from crying. "I appreciate everything you do for them and I know I should be telling you that. I want to do whatever I can to have a special day with Olivia."

That's...not the callous response I was expecting. "I think that's a great idea."

He nods and meets my gaze. I notice the dark circles beneath his eyes for the first time and can't help feeling sympathy for him. He looks like he has the weight of the world on his shoulders.

"Is there...anything else I can help with?" I ask.

He scoffs, a corner of his lips lifting in a smile. "You want to marry me?"

I tilt my head, confused. "Sorry, what?"

He sighs heavily and walks over to the fridge to get some water. Then he comes over to me, speaking in a low tone meant only for the two of us.

"The girls' dad hasn't seen them since Hallie was a baby. He's a complete deadbeat. Never helped Rachel with anything after he left. My attorney told me I should adopt the girls to protect against him coming after them in the future, and he's fighting it. He says he wants full custody--in Alaska, with him and his girlfriend."

My jaw drops. "Alaska? No. You can't let this happen. The girls are already having a hard enough time."

"I know. And I know I'm not...nurturing or whatever, but the girls will always be my priority. I don't date and I don't plan to as long as I'm raising them. I'll do anything to keep them safe and happy."

I'm so floored by the bombshell he just dropped that I don't even react to his assessment of himself as *not nurturing or whatever*. "Why does their father have this sudden interest? Where has he been all these years?"

Carter's gaze darkens. "Money. He wants my sister's life insurance money."

"I'm not a violent person, but I'm feeling very violent at this moment."

"Yeah, I felt the same way when I heard. My attorney told me I need to have my aunt come for a weekend visit as soon as possible to beef up my case that I have family around, and that if I have a girl-friend I've considered marrying, now is the time."

"What? No! Carter, you can't marry some random woman the girls don't even know. That's--"

I gesture wildly, unable to think of a strong enough word.

"I know," he interjects. "That's why I thought of you."

I just gape at him. "You were serious? I thought that was a stressed-out quip."

"I don't know what else to do. Nancy--she's the weekend nanny--she...well, I don't know how to be tactful about it. She has a big hairy mole on her cheek and she's pushing sixty years old. No one would buy me marrying her."

I laugh. "You could tell them she's the only one who will put up with your personality."

He frowns. "I guess the gloves are staying off, then. Great."

I shrug. "The gloves can go back on when you get your shit together."

"Do I seem like I have any hope of that?"

"I mean...not at all."

He sighs softly. "Just give it some thought. I thought about it the whole way home, and it could work. It would just be a marriage on paper to us, but we would have to sell it to everyone else. We could definitely handle that. And the girls love you."

"Right, but it's *marriage*. That's real."

"I'll pay you. A lot. And we can quietly divorce in a year or two--after the adoption is finalized."

I can't help it--the mention of money makes my ears perk up. I'm more than a hundred and eighty thousand dollars in debt, thanks to Tyler and his adult toy disaster.

But the girls. I have to think of the girls. "Don't you think it would be hard for the girls to lose their stepmom when we divorced?"

Carter's expression is grim. "I know, I don't want that for them, either. But I have to go with the best of two imperfect scenarios. Rachel wanted me to raise them if she couldn't. She knew what a douchebag Chad is."

I just look at him, running out of arguments against this *insane* idea.

His tone is imploring when he says, "Think about it, okay? I'll pay you five hundred thousand dollars if you do it. It's not about me or you. It's about the girls. I'd marry a fucking chair to keep them here instead of Alaska."

"You really know how to sweet-talk a girl." I roll my eyes again. "I'll think about it, but...I'll think about it. That's all I'm saying right now. Give me a couple of days."

I can't marry Carter. It's the craziest thing anyone's ever suggested to me.

But...a lot of money is on the line. And more importantly, the futures of the three little girls I've already grown to love.

I have to at least think about it.

CHAPTER SIX

Carter

THIS DAMN PEDICURE CHAIR. I'm too tall for the back of my head to be on the headrest, and it's massaging me so hard my balls are jiggling in my boxer briefs.

But when Olivia looks over at me hopefully, I force a smile and say, "Great idea. This is relaxing."

When I got home this morning to pick her up after I went to practice, she was surprised. And happy. After what Suki told me last night, I would have done anything she asked for to celebrate her birthday. I guess I should be grateful I'm only getting my feet washed and massaged. I could be getting a perm or something.

The pedicure technician picks up one of my feet

and gestures with her chin. I just look at her, unsure what she wants. She does it again.

"I don't know--"

She puts her hand on a stirrup-looking thing and frowns at me.

"You're supposed to put your foot in there," Olivia says, saving me.

She said her mom took her to get a pedicure a couple of times for special occasions, so at least one of us knows what the hell is going on here.

I put my foot up in the thing and then the technician pats the other one, so I follow it with my other foot. She looks at the bottoms of my feet and says something in Vietnamese to the technician doing Olivia's pedicure.

The other woman looks at my feet, shakes her head and says something back. I can tell from their tone that they aren't complimenting me. But whatever. This is for Olivia. I pick up my phone and open my email, trying to ignore the way my balls are vibrating.

I'm sorting out messages that need to be read from ones I can delete when a weird tingle on the bottom of my foot makes me reflexively jerk it upward.

The technician frowns and says something I

don't understand, then pushes my foot back into the stirrup thing.

She runs a flat metal grater over the bottom of my foot and I groan, my foot jerking in reaction again.

Now she's glaring at me. I glare back.

"You have to hold still, Uncle Carter," Olivia says.

"I can't help it."

The customer in the chair on the other side of me is looking at me, and Olivia gives me a *please don't embarrass me* look.

I drop the scowl and say, "Sorry. I'll hold still."

The technician shit-talks me in Vietnamese again, her coworker laughing this time. This is fucking ridiculous. I want to get up and leave.

But it's for Olivia's birthday. So when the technician grates my foot, lighter this time, I force my foot to remain in place. She keeps going, and when she hits a certain spot, it's all I can do not to kick her in the face as I jerk away because it tickles.

"Sorry. It tickles," I explain.

I think both of us are relieved when she puts the grater down. She moves on to clipping my toenails and digging into my nail beds. But pain, I can handle.

When she clips out a big piece of toenail from the side of one of my big toes, she holds the nail up in front of me in the clippers, accusing me of something I don't understand. I just shrug.

"We need to come here more often," Olivia says. "Your feet need a lot of work."

I'd rather chomp on rusty scraps of metal, but instead, I smile like it's the best idea I've ever heard.

The technician massages my feet, her hands working the kind of magic I'm used to on the rest of my body from our team's athletic trainer. This part's definitely not so bad.

Olivia's getting her toenails painted bright pink as my technician massages lotion into my feet. I'm so damn happy when I get to put my shoes back on and pay the bill.

"What did you think?" Olivia asks me as we're walking back to the car.

"Not bad at all. Minus the grater and the jackhammer massage chair, I mean."

"You should have asked her to turn the chair off."

"Yeah."

I check my phone, hoping Leo sent me the text I've been expecting. It's there, and I breathe a sigh of relief. Olivia's surprise gift is taken care of.

"What do you want to do next?" I ask her once we're back in the car.

She shrugs. "That was fun. We can just go back home."

"No way. How about some shopping? And some Starbucks?"

Rachel told me Olivia wanted a Starbucks gift card for her last birthday, so I assume she still likes it. Based on the way she lights up when I mention it, I'm right.

When we get to Starbucks, I get a black coffee and Olivia orders a pink drink.

"This was my mom's favorite here," she says as we sit down at a small table.

Her gaze turns wistful and falls to the cup.

"Rach always liked strawberry shakes when we were kids," I say. "With lots of whipped cream. Our mom used to get mad at us because we'd spray whipped cream right into each other's mouths."

"Really?" Olivia smiles broadly, drinking up the new information about her mom.

"Believe it or not, your mom was usually the mastermind when we'd get in trouble. It was her idea to make our mom's bedroom into a trampoline park for the neighbor kids the first summer our mom let us stay home alone while she was at work. We charged two dollars per kid to come jump on Mom's bed and we sold snacks from our kitchen."

"Did you get in trouble?"

I smile at the memory. "Big time. One of the other kid's parents told our mom and she came home one day when we had about ten kids jumping on her bed. She took us to work with her at the library every day for the rest of the summer and all we could do was sit at a desk and read."

"I don't have any memories of Grandma from before she died, but Mom used to talk about her."

"Rachel was a lot like her." I take a sip of my coffee, remembering my sister's contagious laugh. "I miss them both."

"Me too."

"You remind me of your mom."

Olivia's eyes brighten. "I do? How?"

"The way you like to take care of people, like your sisters."

Her expression turns annoyed. "They don't listen to me."

"Do you feel like you need to help them do things the way your mom would want?"

"Yeah, but Charlotte just gives me attitude. Hallie listens sometimes, I guess."

I shift in my seat, unable to get comfortable. It's new for me, trying to say things to the girls in a soft, sensitive way. You have to be pretty unsoft and insensitive to make it in hockey, where I spend most of my time.

"You know, I'm the one who needs to keep your sisters in line. I like that you've tried to help me with it because I know I'm not the best at some things. I want you to just be a kid. Just focus on you and don't worry about your sisters. Let me do that."

"And Suki."

There's a catch in my chest as I picture the concern on Suki's face last night when I told her about my predicament. She hasn't even been working for me for two months, and already the girls have a strong bond with her. I was still in such a daze from Rachel's death that I mostly ignored her until very recently.

I probably owe her an apology. She was right to rattle my cage a couple of times. I figured she'd laugh and quit when I asked her to marry me last night.

Damn, it sounds so weird to even think the words. I never thought I'd propose to anyone. Even if it wasn't really a proposal as much as a proposition. It took my attorney telling me Chad has an actual chance at taking the girls from me to make me wake the hell up and see things clearly.

"You guys like Suki, don't you?"

Olivia smiles. "Yeah, Suki's awesome. She's always happy and she takes us to do fun things."

I check my watch, remembering Leo's text. "We need to get going. How about a jewelry store? You want to pick out a necklace or something?"

She grins. "Are you serious?"

"Yeah, absolutely."

I look for jewelry stores on my phone and find a locally owned one right off downtown with good online reviews. We've only been talking to our salesperson, Julia, for about a minute when an older man in a shirt and tie approaches us.

"Mr. Stanton, thank you for coming in. I'm Bill McKay, the owner. If there's anything at all I can do to help, don't hesitate to ask."

I feel a flicker of annoyance, though it's irrational. Being recognized in my team's town happens often. Today, though, it feels like someone intruding on my time with my niece.

"Thanks, man." I shake his extended hand. "I appreciate it."

"I've had Crush season tickets for the past twelve years. My wife and I are big fans."

"We appreciate that. I brought my niece in to pick out a gift."

Bill looks at Olivia and smiles. "If there's anything we can do to help, just let us know. We'll let you look."

My irritation fades with his acknowledgment of her. Rachel would balk over me bringing her eleven-year-old here to choose her own gift, but I'm going with my gut on this one. This birthday is special.

Olivia is wide-eyed as she scans the jewelry in

every single case before making her choice. When Julia asked her if she wanted something with a topaz, the birthstone for November, she asked about the February birthstone, Rachel's birth month.

When Julia fastens Olivia's new amethyst necklace around her neck, I have to swallow against the lump in my throat. The girls have told me Suki asks them about their mom all the time, and at first it annoyed me because I thought she was just pouring salt in their wounds.

I see it now, though. Olivia is beaming as we leave the store. Remembering Rachel today has made it easier for her, not harder.

Suki is a lot more than just a beautiful face. She's amazing with the girls. I hope like hell she accepts my offer.

"Now I've got a surprise for you," I tell Olivia when we're back in the car.

"Uncle Carter, no. This is already so much." She gently touches her new necklace. "I love this. You don't need to get me anything else."

"I already did. We're going to pick it up. It's going to be a long drive, though. Like an hour and a half."

"That's okay." She gets her phone out of her tiny purse. "I have a playlist we can listen to."

"That sounds great."

Eighty-eight minutes and a shitload of Taylor

Swift songs later, we pull into the driveway of a house in the country.

Olivia gives me a confused look. "We're at someone's house."

"Yep."

I put my Range Rover in park and text the man Leo sent contact information for.

"You'll need your coat. We're meeting him in a building out back."

When I see a guy in a heavy flannel and a baseball hat walking toward us, I get out of the car. Olivia follows, coming around to stand next to me.

"Carter?" the man asks me.

"That's me." I shake his hand.

"I'm John. You guys ready to pick out a pig?"

Olivia is still confused, but when we walk into an outbuilding and she sees around a half dozen tiny pink pigs curled up around each other in the hay, her jaw drops.

"A pet pig? Uncle Carter! Really?"

I nod. "Pick one out."

Her expression is so thrilled that I grab my phone and take a picture of it. When she sits down in the hay on the ground of the pen, two of the pigs go right to her, snuffing and snorting.

She laughs and picks one up, cradling it. It squeals like she's stabbing it.

"They're dramatic," John says. "She's fine."

It doesn't take Olivia long to choose one. It's a pink male with no spots, and I swear he looks like he's smiling at her.

I owe Leo for this. At practice this morning, I asked him to find me a tiny pet piglet as quickly as possible. He came through.

I send John his payment over Venmo and he sends us with some hay and pellet food to get us started. Olivia's happiness on the ride home makes me feel, for the first time since Rachel died, like we're going to do more than just survive.

If we can stay together, that is. Suki will have a lot to do with that. All I can do now is hope she makes the right choice.

CHAPTER SEVEN

Suki

"Okay, first pro--he has a big dick."

I gape at Dex, who is sitting in between Mara and Harry on my couch, writing on a legal pad. "What? How do you know that?"

"Oh, honey. It took less than half an hour of YouTube videos to find an interview of him in a locker room with a visible dick outline."

Mara bites her lip. "Was he still sweaty? I have a thing for sweaty dicks."

Dex and Harry both cringe dramatically.

"First of all." Dex puts up a hand. "By the time the dick itself is sweaty, there is an entire ecosystem growing in a man's crotch region."

Mara rolls her eyes. "You guys are prudes. I love a big, strong, sweaty man."

"Guys." Standing on the other side of the couch, I glare at them. "Can we stay on topic here? This is a life-changing decision for me. And it has nothing to do with Carter's dick size because it would be a marriage on paper only."

"Okay, sorry." Dex, an attorney, always helps me make pro/con lists when I'm feeling indecisive. He's Rory Gilmore in the form of an attractive gay man. "I crossed off big dick, though as your attorney, I feel you should consider it."

"Do I need an attorney for this?"

He considers. "If you decide to do it, yes. But I've got you. I'll need to review the contract terms before you sign anything. And I mean *anything*, Suki."

I sigh heavily, walking over to the coffee table to pick up one of the bacon-wrapped dates Harry included on the big tray of appetizers he brought over for our pro/con session. Even though he's a chef who cooks a solid fifty hours a week at his restaurant, Harry never misses a chance to cook for us.

"This is crazy though, right?" I ask as I chew. "I mean...I can't marry someone I hardly even know just for money."

"It's a lot of money, though," Mara reminds me.

My shoulders sink with defeat. For them to fully understand this decision, I have to confess my shameful secret to Dex and Harry.

"Okay, it's *listen and don't judge* time. I cosigned all of Tyler's loans for his business. So now that he's gone, I'm...a hundred and eighty-three thousand four hundred and eighty-six dollars in debt." I furrow my brow. "Ish. I don't know if my last payment has cleared."

Harry clamps a hand over his mouth. "Holy shit, Suki."

"Un. Fucking. Real." Dex gives me a stunned look. "Why the hell--"

"I did it, okay?" I keep my voice brisk and to the point. "I don't want to hear about how dumb it was. I obviously already know."

I can tell it takes considerable effort for him to press his lips together and stay quiet.

I curl up in my favorite old recliner. "I was such an idiot. But now you know why Carter offering me five hundred thousand dollars for this marriage really would change my life. My credit is destroyed. The loans are the reason I'm working two jobs, but I can barely keep up with the payments."

Mara leans forward, picking up a plate to load up with appetizers. "I don't know if this helps or not, but I'd do it. Carter is gone most of the time and you love those girls. So it's basically just a massive raise for the next year of work. I owe about ninety-five grand on law school and college loans, and if I could pay them back by marrying a pro athlete for a year, I'd do it in a second. As long as he doesn't abuse you or expect sex, you've got nothing to lose."

"I'd do it, too," Dex says.

I look at Harry, who shrugs. "I don't know. You know me, I'm a romantic."

He really is. Harry is tall and blond with a killer smile. He's a chef and an artist who doesn't jump in and out of relationships. He and Dex were a couple for around five months a few years ago before deciding they were better off as friends.

"I'm already at his house a lot, but moving in feels..." I can't even finish the sentence, because I don't know how to describe the way it feels. "And I'd have to make it look like I'm in love with him." My laugh is tinged with disbelief. "How could I possibly sell that? He's the opposite of my type."

Mara says, "Well, your type did fuck you over and leave the country, so..."

I wince at the sharp reminder of my stupidity, then shake my head. "Tyler wasn't my type, either."

Mara laughs--a hard, long laugh that ends with her wiping tears from the corners of her eyes. "He was *exactly* your type. Charismatic, charming, making everything, including himself, sound better than it really was--"

"That's not my type."

She looks at Harry and Dex. Dex widens his eyes and Harry stares intently at his nails.

"Harry?" I give him a look, expecting him to jump to my defense.

He starts coughing. It's clearly fake, but he scrunches up his face and pats his chest, standing up from the couch. "Sorry, I need to get some water."

I turn to Dex. "Well?"

He blows out a long, dramatic exhale. "I love you, but you do tend to go for charming liars."

I glare between him and Mara, getting up to make a plate of carb-loaded comfort food. "You guys, it's not like men introduce themselves by letting you know they're liars. How is anyone supposed to know that up front?"

"Tyler was slicker than my cooch anytime Jeffrey Dean Morgan was on *The Walking Dead*," Mara says.

"Girl." Dex puts his palm up for a high five without even looking at her. "The things I would let that man do to me."

I'm not even done loading up my plate, but I set it on the table and stand up. "Once again, this is not a joke and it's *not about you*. We're supposed to be talking about whether I'm going to get married.

Married. I'll be a divorcée for the rest of my life when it's over."

"A debt-free divorcée with a nice fat bank account, though," Mara says.

"Right. Is that enough of a reason to do it?"

Harry answers as he walks back in from the kitchen. "That's for you to decide, babe. Mara and Dex would do it and I...don't know about me. I might, but I can't be sure."

I sigh softly. "The money would be amazing, but I'm also really attached to the girls. If I don't do this and they have to move to Alaska and live with their dad...it would be really hard on them."

"But there's no guarantee of anything," Dex reminds me. "You don't know for sure that if you do marry him, they'll get to stay here, and you don't know that if you don't marry him, they'll have to go to Alaska."

"But what do you guys think?" I look between Dex and Mara. "As attorneys, do you agree with the advice Carter's attorney gave him?"

Mara shakes her head. "I'm not qualified to give you an opinion on that."

I laugh. "But you have an opinion on literally everything else? Even *my socks*."

She shrugs.

Dex considers before answering. "Michelle

Maroni is the best family law attorney in the Cleveland area. She's an absolute legend. If she thinks it's a good move for him, it is."

"But that doesn't mean you have to be the one he marries," Harry points out.

I walk across the small room and back again, thinking. "I don't want to be in debt for the next decade or more. And if I don't do it, I'll lose my job as Carter's nanny. If he has to show the girls aren't being raised by nannies, he can't keep me." I take a breath in and out, my heart racing as I realize which direction I'm leaning. "I love the girls, too. I can't stand the thought of some stranger marrying him for the money and treating them like crap. So I guess..."

Mara jumps up from the couch, clapping and squealing. "My best friend is gonna be a pro hockey wife!"

"Are you sure?" Dex asks me.

I nod, imagining Olivia, Charlotte and Hallie's expressions when we tell them the news. It makes me smile. "I'm sure."

"Then we have a wedding to plan!" He looks over at Harry. "Gay man party-planning superpowers, activate!"

"We'll have to do it indoors, obviously," Harry

says. "I'm thinking fall neutrals? Bring the outdoors in?"

"Perfect." Dex flips to a fresh page in his notebook, the pro/con list forgotten. "We'll need to go dress shopping immediately and secure hair, nail and makeup appointments."

"You guys, this isn't going to be a real wedding," I remind them. "We just do a quick formality at the courthouse."

Dex and Harry laugh.

"Have you met us?" Dex asks. "No fucking way are we letting our girl have some dreary pantsuit wedding at a courthouse."

"No fucking way," Harry seconds. "You'll have at least a hundred dozen flowers, the best food money can buy and a tiara."

"Maybe a vintage pearl one," Dex says, writing in his notebook as he says it.

"I don't know if Carter will want any of this."

Mara scoffs. "Don't give him a choice."

"Because it'll be so great to marry a guy who's scowling at me during the ceremony."

"Trust me, if you tell him he doesn't have to do a thing but show up and pay the bills, he'll be thrilled."

"Tuxes." Dex is still talking while writing. "We need to know if he has one and we'll need bridesmaid dresses for all the girls."

"And me, asshole," Mara says.

"Wait, bridesmaids?" I silently plead with Mara for help on this one. "I think that's a bit much."

"The girls will want to be part of it," Harry says.

"It also significantly ups my chances of hooking up with a groomsman if I'm the maid of honor, so...definitely bridesmaids," Mara says.

I can't argue with that. Still, the wedding plans are growing by the second, and I haven't even told Carter yet that I'll marry him.

I shake my head and sit down. "I hope this is the right decision."

Mara comes over and bends down in front of the chair, so we're eye level with each other.

"You know me. I'd never tell you to do this just so I could hook up with a hockey player. This is a chance for you to get out of debt and leave all that shit with Tyler behind you forever. For five hundred Gs, I'd do a lot worse than marry a pro athlete for a year."

I blow out a breath, thinking about prying the quarters that were my tip out of dried, spilled beer during my last waitressing shift at the bar. Coming home exhausted at 1:00 a.m., smelling like fries and having to get up for my day job the next day. Mara is right--this will hardly change anything with my day job, and it will mean no more second job and years of scraping to pay off Tyler's loans. All I have to do is move into Carter's house and convince people I love him.

"Okay." I nod, feeling more confident. "Dex, we're also going to need a tux for a pig."

He doesn't look up from his legal pad. "Groom's is already on my list, babe."

I smile. "No, not him. An actual pig. Carter got the girls a micro pig for a pet. They'll want him to be part of the ceremony."

"Put a photographer on your list," Mara tells Dex. "I have a feeling this wedding will be something we all look back on later and laugh about."

I wonder again if I'm making a huge mistake. If I am, at least I'll have my closest friends by my side as I formalize it.

CHAPTER EIGHT

Carter

"Uncle Carter, look at Darling!"

Hallie holds up the pig she won an argument with Olivia about naming. He's officially Darling Maxwell Stanton now.

Just a few months ago my house was empty other than me. Today, it's full of people. There's a pink two-tier cake in my dining room, my wife-to-be is getting ready in my bedroom and I have a pet pig wearing a tuxedo.

"What the hell, man?" Bash speaks out of the corner of his mouth, his smile still in place. "We need to alk-tay right ow-nay."

I roll my eyes at his pig latin. My teammates were

understandably shocked when I announced after practice yesterday that I was getting married today. I told them Suki and I had a secret whirlwind courtship. Knowing how opposed I am to even being in a relationship, Bash is convinced I'm being framed or something.

"Carter, the photographer needs you." Suki's friend Dex, our volunteer wedding planner, is a dead ringer for the actor Tom Holland. "She wants some photos of just you and then just you and the girls."

I hold back a shitty comment about hating photos, nodding instead. Suki's friends are taking this wedding way too seriously. In the back of my mind, I'm wondering if she might have a thing for me that they know about. If they think there's any chance we'll actually fall for each other, they couldn't be more wrong.

I hate everything about this. The stuffy tux, the fussing...the damned bills. This rush wedding for show is costing me a mint. I'm also missing the Penn State football game.

The one thing I don't hate is how happy the girls are. I've never seen them as excited as they were when Suki and I told them we were getting married. Olivia was confused at first. Since she's old enough to see that we have no chemistry and never spend time alone together. But even she's on board now, looking older than her age in her pale-pink dress, her hair styled in waves around her shoulders.

She latched onto Suki's friends immediately--especially Mara. Olivia and Hallie were deadlocked in a fight about the pig's name. I told them when we brought him home that he belonged equally to all three of them even though Olivia picked him out. Charlotte suggested we name him Bacon but didn't care when everyone dismissed the idea.

It was Mara who told Olivia it would be cool for her to let the youngest sister name their pet, and Olivia immediately agreed.

"Hey." Bash grabs my arm as I start to walk away.

I turn and look at him. "I'm good, man. I swear. I'm the one who asked her to marry me."

"Yeah, but there's legal stuff, and--"

He's worried I don't have a prenup. Little does he know the amount of back-and-forth between Dex and Michelle over the contract Suki and I signed spelling out the terms of this union.

"It's taken care of. I promise."

He shakes his head. "You're insane. But don't say I didn't try to talk some sense into you."

"I have to go get pictures done."

I walk away, knowing he's right. This *is* insane. But Chad has me backed into a corner, and this could be my only hope of keeping custody of the girls. Aunt Rosie is coming this weekend, when I have a rare Friday and Saturday night off, to stay with the girls so Suki and I can have a quick "honeymoon."

That'll be awkward as fuck, but I guess we should complete the charade.

The photographer poses me and the girls in front of the fireplace, the pig squealing in Charlotte's arms like he's being tortured.

"Charlotte, ditch the pig," I say.

"No, he's part of our family."

The photographer snaps a photo I'll definitely look pissed off in. We only have around a dozen guests and all of them are staring at us right now.

"Do you want me to hold him?" Leo offers.

"No," Hallie answers. "I'll take him. He loves me. He's my darling."

I swear the pig has put on five pounds already, and we just got him a few days ago. With her little hands, she can barely hold him. She wraps her arms around his midsection, his squeals getting louder as his legs hang down.

"Give me the damn pig," I say wearily.

She passes him to me and I cradle him, trying to smile as the pig snorts and roots its nose around on my face. Bash and Leo are standing near the photographer, both taking their own photos. Fuckers.

Dex claps his hands. "Okay, we'll have to finish up photos later. It's time to move into our positions for the ceremony."

My blood pressure ticks upward as I go to the small *X* Dex made for me with painter's tape. My living room is large, but it still feels like a tight fit for a dozen guests, me, Bash and Leo, the girls, the pig and the flower arch thing.

I tug on the collar of my dress shirt. At least Bash and Leo are standing up here with me, both of them in suits because there wasn't enough time for them to get fitted for tuxes.

I go to so many charity dinners that I own a tux. Fortunately, it still fits well even though I've been stepping up my arm and shoulder workouts this season.

My dress shoes feel tight and I'm sweating. The string quartet Dex hired starts up and I square my shoulders. I have to make it look like I actually want to be here right now, even though I wanted to exchange vows at the courthouse and be done with it.

Our handful of guests stand as Suki walks down the stairs. Once she turns the corner, I get my first look at her since yesterday. She's on her friend Harry's arm, her expression a perfect mixture of nervous and serene.

I, on the other hand, turn anything but serene, like a switch was just flipped inside me. She's wearing a long, sleeveless, off-white dress with pearls sewn into the bodice and skirt in intricate, swirling designs. It hugs every one of her curves I've never paid attention to until this moment.

She's not just beautiful--she's stunning. Her hair is styled simply in a thick knot at her neck, a delicate tiara atop her head. Though her everyday look is very little makeup, today she looks like she belongs in a fashion magazine, the green in her eyes highlighted by her dramatic eye makeup.

My pulse is pounding like it does in anticipation of a high-stakes game. This isn't real, but it's still fucking with my head. That's my future *wife* walking toward me.

Harry smiles at me when they reach the end of their short walk. Suki passes Mara her small bouquet of flowers and I catch a glimpse of the back of her dress, which is open all the way to the top of her waist. Fuck me, even her back is sexy.

She reaches for me and I take her much smaller hands in mine.

Our officiant starts the ceremony and I hear his words, but they don't really sink in. I can't look at or think about anything but Suki right now. She's glowing. I feel an urge to reach over and cup the back of her bare neck and pull her closer.

That's crazy. I'm just caught up in the moment. I have to stay focused.

Dex wrote our short, to-the-point vows. I look into her eyes as I recite mine, the depth of promising to love and honor one woman *forever* hitting me even though I'm not really doing it.

I'm not made that way. My dad broke his promises to my mom and I saw what it did to her. I won't do that to anyone, ever.

Suki does her vows perfectly, even promising to love and be there for the girls forever. I feel her sincerity. We talked about things alone last night and she asked for my promise that even when we end this fake marriage, she can still have a close relationship with the girls.

My sister's death was a brutal twist of fate. I'm so damn lucky the nanny agency happened to send me someone who genuinely cares about my nieces.

Surprisingly, Charlotte is the only one of the girls who gets emotional during the ceremony. She wipes a tear from the corner of her eye and the gravity of all this sets in.

I'm not a bachelor anymore. I can't fuck around with women I meet on the road and party with my single teammates. Even though Suki and I won't be together forever, the girls and I will. I'm as close as I'll ever get to being a dad--to three girls. Boys, I can handle, but girls?

As they grow into adolescence without their mom around, the roller coaster ride we're all on will probably get more intense.

Bash pokes me as the officiant says, "You may kiss your bride," while giving me a look that conveys it's not the first time he's said it.

I put my game face on, grinning at Suki as I gently cup her cheek and lean in to kiss her. Her lips are soft and she tastes like mint. I put my free hand on her hip and squeeze gently, eliciting a little moan from her.

Damn. Is she inexperienced? Or just nervous? I like the way she lets me lead, her eyes wide when I pull back slightly. In another time and place, I'd want to do more than just kiss her right now.

"Ladies and gentlemen, Mr. and Mrs. Carter Stanton," the officiant announces proudly.

Everyone claps. Well, everyone besides Darling, who's squealing bloody murder.

Coach Turner held him for the ceremony, and he's eager to get rid of him. Once he's back on the ground, Darling waddles over to the girls, his nose to the ground.

Bash hugs Suki and smiles broadly at her. "I don't

know what you see in him, but welcome to the family."

She glances at me and smiles. "Thank you."

The photographer takes more photos of me and Suki, and then a bunch more of us with the girls. It's going to be weird seeing these photos later, with Suki and I giving each other tender looks even though we hardly know each other.

I feel a stab of guilt every time someone congratulates us. Suki seems genuinely happy. Her friends are thrilled. What if she's catching feelings? If she falls for me, she's going to end up heartbroken. If there's anything I can do to prevent that, I will.

"Hey, can we talk alone?" I ask her.

She furrows her brow. "Right now?"

"Right now."

Leo laughs from nearby and comes over to her, putting an arm around her shoulders. "Don't worry, he just wants to consummate this thing. Won't take him more than a minute, minute and a half tops, from what I've heard."

I scowl, not in the mood for his antics. Suki excuses herself and follows me upstairs to my bedroom. Once we're inside with the door closed behind us, I tear off the annoying as fuck bow tie and unbutton the top button on my shirt.

Able to breathe again, I sit down on the edge of the bed, unsure how to approach this conversation.

"So how are you feeling?" I ask tentatively.

She sighs softly, sitting down on the leather chair in the corner. "Glad the hard part's behind us. What about you? You seem extra broody."

I bristle. "I'm not broody."

"You're literally brooding right this second."

"How am I brooding?"

"Your expression, your tone...it's a whole vibe, and the vibe is broody."

Dammit. I just signed up to have a woman giving me her commentary about me all the time.

I decide to just be straight with her. "Okay, look. You seemed really happy during the ceremony and I just want to make sure we're still on the same page."

She hikes up her brows. "The same page?"

"I'm not going to fall in love with you."

Her immediate laugh is full-throated and it lasts longer than it should. I seethe inside over her amusement at what I just said.

"Don't worry about that," she finally says, wiping a corner of her eye.

I sit up straight, unbuttoning a cuff of my shirt. "I'm trying to be a good guy, Suki. I don't want you to end up...hurt and disappointed."

She huffs out a single note of unamused laughter. "Thanks, but I'd rather walk naked down on the side of a busy highway than be in another relationship. I'm doing this for the girls and the money. Full stop."

"You don't have to be so dramatic. I'm not that bad."

"It's not about you. I know you aren't used to hearing that."

I keep my cool as I unbutton my other cuff and roll up the sleeve of my shirt. "I just wanted to be a clear communicator. Your friends are all really happy for you and I thought you might be having some feelings."

Another laugh. Honestly, I'm offended by the laughing at this point. "Oh, I'm having some feelings, all right. But not like you're thinking. And my friends are happy for me because of the money. They know this is all fake and they're just playing their parts."

"You told them?"

She wrinkles her nose, confused. "Yeah, I had to. They wouldn't have believed I was marrying you because I just wanted to."

I stand up, a muscle in my jaw ticcing with annoyance. "I'm done with this conversation. I'm going back downstairs."

"Okay, I'll be down soon. I'm going to change out

of this dress. I don't want to get food on it because I'm planning to sell it."

I guess that's that. I'll admit to some brooding as I leave the room. Apparently, my flicker of attraction toward her was a one-sided thing. It's for the best. This fake marriage is going to be complicated enough without feelings for each other in the mix.

CHAPTER NINE

Suki

"I THINK THAT WENT WELL. How about you?"

Carter gives me a questioning look after closing the door to his--now our--bedroom. I nod, the day catching up with me all at once as I slide out of the heels I wore with the casual dress I changed into after the ceremony.

"About as well as it could have," I agree absently.

"Other than Darling shitting in the middle of the dining room three times. And you telling everyone the marriage isn't real."

I sigh softly, flexing my sore feet. "You know, if you could make shitty comments like fifty or sixty percent of the time instead of a hundred, that would be really nice."

He scoffs as he unbuttons his dress shirt. "I'm not being shitty. I told you how important it is that we sell this as a real relationship. If it gets out that I'm trying to play games with the judge in the custody case, that'll be a big fucking problem. Michelle was clear about that."

"I only told my three closest friends in the world. They probably would've had me involuntarily committed if I told them I was marrying a man I hardly knew. All I've said to them about you before this is that you're kind of cold and selfish."

His jaw drops as he takes off his dress shirt and walks over to the massive walk-in closet. "What the fuck, Suki? That's what you think of me?"

Yikes. Probably shouldn't have told him that. "Only sometimes. And you've gotten better. But let's stay on topic. I'm not telling my family or anyone else the truth. So don't worry. I won't do anything to put the custody case in jeopardy. I want the best for the girls."

He walks into the closet, leaving me in silence. I glance around the room, which is dimly lit by built-in sconces over each bedside table and ceiling lights over the bed. When I was getting ready for the ceremony earlier, I discovered that this bedroom has seven different light switches. The closet has another three and the bathroom has five. That's more than my entire apartment.

Carter's house was furnished and decorated by a pro. And his bedroom is more masculine than the rest of it. The furniture is all dark and sturdy, the walls painted a soft gray. A huge, expensive-looking rug covers the dark wood flooring. His king-sized bed has a beautiful arched wood headboard and it's made neatly with a white duvet and a few decorative pillows.

Did he do that? His house cleaner, Andrea, comes twice a week and cleans for a few hours each time, but today wasn't one of her days. I can imagine fussy Carter arranging his pillows just so, his brows lowered in judgment of the alignment.

There's a sitting area with two leather chairs arranged in front of a small fireplace, a small table between the chairs stacked with a few hardback books. I walk over and look at them, wondering if they're really books he's read or just decorative.

They're all biographies. Warren Buffet, George Washington and Billie Jean King.

"You guys should come to the game tomorrow night." Carter walks out of the closet and I glance over at him as he speaks.

I have to force it to be a glance because he doesn't

have a shirt on. He's only wearing black athletic shorts. And I've never seen a man with a body like his this close up. Tyler's Cheetos and Fruity Pebbles addictions kept his abs so well hidden I never saw them. Carter, on the other hand, likes to snack on grilled chicken and cucumber.

"Sure, I know the girls have been dying to go to one," I say, keeping my tone casual.

"The counselor I'm working with said I should wait until I think they're ready for questions about their mom. Even though my teammates and their families know better than to ask about her, there's always that random nosy asshole who could say something."

This is a two-way conversation, and I can't be part of it and not look at him. But I don't want to get busted ogling his muscles, so I keep my gaze on his face as I respond.

"If anybody says anything in front of me, they'll feel my wrath."

Carter grins. "You have a wrath?"

"I do."

"I can kind of see that. When we first met, I thought you were just a sweet, passive, pretty face who likes everyone and everything."

My heart skips a beat over him calling me pretty. Must be biological because I'm not into him. At the same time, I scoff at his comment, though it does hit home. Past Suki was way too sweet and passive, and look where it got me. Burned and buried in debt by a man who took advantage of me.

Never again.

"You thought wrong. I stand up for myself, and I'll stand up to anyone who tries to hurt the girls."

"Good."

I flash him a quick smile. "Remember you said that when I stand up to *you*."

A corner of his lips quirks up in a sexy smile. "I don't want you to be a doormat, Suki. For this to work, we have to be completely open with each other."

"I agree."

"I want you and the girls at all my home games, even if you have to leave early on school nights."

I furrow my brow. "Okay, I don't like the way you commanded it, but I'll do my best."

He starts taking the decorative pillows off the bed, stacking them on one of the leather chairs. "My team shirts and sweaters are in the closet in one of the drawers by the door. The light-blue one on the bottom is the one I'd give to my wife, so wear that one."

I get a fluttering sensation in my stomach. His

wife. I don't know if I'll ever get used to the sound of that.

Wearing his clothes feels very intimate. But I guess he's right. It's probably something I'd do if we were really a couple.

"You said it's a sweater?"

"A jersey. We call them sweaters."

"Oh."

"I'll have someone from the front office bring over some stuff for the girls to wear tomorrow."

My gaze starts to drift down to his defined chest, which has hair a shade lighter than the hair on his head and face. His shoulders and chest also have a few freckles. I check myself, forcing my eyes back to his.

"If that...sweater is important to you, I don't want to risk ruining it."

"You'll be fine. It's already got a rip in one arm from the game I wore it in."

"You only wore it once?"

He nods. "I wore it when my team won the championship my second year in the pros."

I clear my throat, unsure what to say. "I'll, um, see how it looks on me tomorrow."

He's done with the pillows. There are only two left on the bed, one on each side, both with crisp-looking white pillowcases.

"Wear it," he orders.

I bristle at his no-nonsense tone over what I'll be wearing. I never signed over this level of control to him.

"Look, just because your past girlfriends have all been vapid groupies who wept over wearing your jersey, that doesn't mean I'm doing it." I fold my arms to emphasize my point.

"My last girlfriend was a professor of archaeology at NYU. It's been a long fucking day and I have another long fucking day tomorrow, so can you just give me a break on this one so we can go to bed?"

I hate his tone, but I'm tired, too. I'm also feeling properly chastised over calling his last girlfriend a vapid groupie. "Fine. Can you please undo the top two buttons on this dress for me?"

He approaches, and it's impossible to keep my gaze on just his face. He's just so *big*. I can feel his warmth as I turn around, moving my hair over one shoulder so he can access the buttons I had Mara fasten for me earlier.

The brush of his fingers on my skin makes my heart race. No one said my vow of celibacy after Tyler screwed me over would be easy. Even when we were together, Tyler and I didn't have much sex, so it's been a long time since a man touched me.

"Did you invite your family for Thanksgiving?"

Carter's warm breath is a light caress on my neck as he makes quick work of the buttons.

"No, but I will."

Thanksgiving is in less than two weeks. Carter wants us to host my family and his aunt Rosie, so I have a lot of planning to do. Fortunately, Harry is going to help me with the cooking and Mara and Dex will help with everything else.

"Three brothers, right?" Carter asks as he walks back over to the bed.

I clutch the fabric of my halter-cut dress tightly as I walk over to the closet so it doesn't fall down.

"Right. Jack, Nate and Sean."

Carter gets in bed. "I'm great with brothers."

I'll let him find out for himself how protective my older brothers are and how less than thrilled they and my parents are going to be about our supposed whirlwind courtship and the wedding they weren't invited to. There just wasn't enough time, and I knew my family would have been so alarmed at the idea of me marrying someone they'd never even met that they would have come flying here to stop us.

Someday I'll be able to tell them the truth. Maybe. I'm too ashamed over what Tyler did to me to let my parents in on it. I also want to keep my brothers out of jail.

I have two suitcases full of clothes that I packed earlier, and I dig through one for a pair of light pajama pants and a gray cami to sleep in. I put on a lightweight sports bra beneath the cami, because nips.

It feels great to finally take off my makeup and let my hair down. I already chose one of the two sinks in Carter's bathroom to make mine and lined up my toiletries on the counter. As I brush my teeth, I run my hands through the thick waves of my hair. After being wrapped into a knot for many hours, it's looking pretty unruly.

Taming my hair is a tomorrow thing. Right now, I just want to sleep.

When I walk back into the bedroom, Carter is sitting up on his side of the bed, looking at me over the rim of his reading glasses, a paperback in his hands.

It's *The Immortal Life of Henrietta Lacks*. I feel like an asshole for assuming Carter would only read books about white male athletes, like him. Clearly there's more to him than I thought.

"Can you add me to your health insurance tomorrow?" I ask as I get into bed.

His sheets are silky soft and his bed is very firm but super comfortable. This must be what beds at luxury hotels are like. My bed at home sags in the middle.

"Yep. We've got a good dental plan, too."

I get situated, then switch off the light on my side of the bed.

"Will the light bother you if I read a little longer?" he asks.

"No, not at all."

After a pause, he says, "Hey, I'm not used to sharing a bed with anyone. If I accidentally kick you in the night or something, just kick me back."

"It's a huge bed. I think we'll be okay."

"Yeah."

I turn onto my side, facing away from him. I'm feeling more nervous than I expected over the two of us sharing a bed.

I wonder if the archaeologist ever slept here? Oh God. He probably banged her here. That's a weird feeling.

I can handle discomfort for five hundred thousand dollars, though. He'll be gone a lot of the time for road trips, and this will get easier. As long as we're both adults about it, this is all going to be fine.

Just fine. I tell myself that on repeat to calm my racing heart as I try to fall asleep, running my fingertip over the diamond on my wedding ring.

CHAPTER TEN

Carter

"I FUCKIN' hate those guys." Our goalie Isaac tosses his jock back into his locker. "Bunch of hosers."

We're playing Montreal tonight, and Isaac is still salty about the last time we played them, which was at their arena. Our equipment manager stacked all our equipment bags outside the visiting team locker room there and some Montreal players fucked with Isaac's equipment.

They covered his jock with Vaseline, and no amount of cleaning got all of it off.

"I heard Mariano's getting divorced," Bash says.

Montreal's team captain is actually a really

decent guy. I played with him for about two months at the start of my career.

"No shit?" I say.

"Yeah, I don't know anything else about it."

"I'll have to text him and see if we can catch up sometime."

"You gonna give him some marriage advice? With your twenty-four hours of experience?"

"Yeah, what's up with that?" Isaac asks. "You never mention this woman at all and now you're *married*?"

"Whirlwind courtship," I say, sitting down with my stick and a roll of tape.

"She's his nanny," Bash explains.

"Ah. Okay." Isaac grins.

I scowl at him. "What's that supposed to mean?"

"Nothing. I get it. My sister's nanny is hot as fuck."

"Whatever, man. Suki and the girls are coming to the game tonight, so don't be an asshole to her."

He looks offended. "When am I ever an asshole to women?"

"Only when you're dating them," Leo quips.

Isaac flips him off and turns back to me. "Suki, huh? Is that an Asian name?"

"She's named after her great-grandma, who's Japanese."

It's one of the few personal details I know about Suki. We're both working on lists about ourselves for each other that we can study on our fake honeymoon this weekend.

"Wonder if anyone ever pronounces it *sucky*," Leo ponders aloud.

"I'm sure emotionally immature dipshits like you can't resist the urge," I say.

My phone is sitting next to me on the bench, and I pick it up when the screen lights up with a new text. It's a photo from Suki of the girls, all three of them smiling and wearing Crush sweaters. Charlotte is holding Darling, who's wearing a little Crush hoodie, the sleeves rolled up to accommodate his short legs.

From the background of the photo, I can tell they're in the family room, where our families and close friends can go before and after games. There are snacks, drinks and games for kids. The team even has childcare there for young kids who aren't interested in the games.

For fuck's sake, that damn pig is smiling again. I close my eyes for a second, then text Suki back.

Carter: You brought the pig??

Suki: I had to. He got into the pantry earlier and made a huge mess. He spilled Cheerios everywhere and got into some other food. There's nowhere I can keep him where I know he won't ruin anything.

Carter: I can't believe you got through security with him.

Suki: I told them he's yours. The security guys are the ones who gave him the hoodie.

Carter: How's his house-training going?

Suki: Not great. He peed once on our walk earlier, but he peed three times in the house. One of those times was on your shoes that were in the laundry room.

Carter: What an asshole.

Suki: The girls are feeding him cupcakes. He's had three in the past three minutes. I better go.

I set my phone back down, then pick it back up and look at the picture she sent me. Darling is growing like crazy. I swear he's put on ten pounds and we haven't even had him for two weeks.

Several teammates are laughing, and when I glance over at them, I see that Bash is part of the group, and he's looking right at me.

"Bro, you didn't mention that your new wife sells sex toys. Has she introduced you to the anal invader yet?"

I furrow my brow. "What the fuck are you talking about?"

Bash grabs Silas's phone from his hand and

brings it over. "Some hockey blogger wrote about you getting married. He's got a photo of the marriage license and stuff he dug up online about Suki."

I take the phone and read the post, which includes several photos taken from Suki's social media and lists Olivia, Charlotte and Hallie by name. There are also photos of her with a man named Tyler McCane, and business paperwork for a company called Naughty by Nature.

Fuck. If this is legit, what have I done? I'll be the laughingstock of the league. Parents of the kids at the girls' schools will see this. And it sure as hell won't help my custody case.

But I can't let on to my teammates that I'm shocked by this. I keep my expression neutral as I pass the phone back to Bash.

"Yeah, she doesn't do much with the company anymore."

He just looks at me as I pass the phone back. I know him well enough that I can tell what he's thinking. He's my best friend. Not only is he wondering whether or not I knew about this, but he also realizes it's not something to laugh about when the custody case hangs in the balance.

"Let us know how you like taking the Shake n' Quake up your poop chute, Stanton!" Silas says, poring over his own phone screen with several teammates.

"Jesus fuck." Isaac looks at the screen. "For a hundred and fifty-nine dollars, that thing better do more than just get people off. You could get like ten handies for that."

Bash takes Silas's phone back to him, not laughing anymore. As soon as Silas opens his mouth to make another comment, Bash silences him with a look.

"Move on," he says.

He comes over to the bench and sits down beside me, not saying anything for a solid thirty seconds.

"Did you know?" he asks.

"Yeah," I lie. "I didn't ask for details, but she told me."

"Okay, good."

I keep taping my stick, hoping he won't notice the tic in my jaw. That and a reddening face are dead giveaways that I'm seriously pissed, and Bash knows it.

"You good?" he asks me.

"Yep."

I'm not. He gets up, leaving me alone with my thoughts.

Suki is part owner of a sex toy company. She

should have told me. And who the fuck is Tyler McCane? Am I getting scammed?

Suki thinks I'm cold and brooding now, but she has no idea how pissed I'll be if she puts the custody case in jeopardy. My nieces are the last pieces of my sister in this world, and they were more precious to her than anyone.

I have to get it together so I can focus on the game, but tonight, Suki and I are going to talk.

———

AT LEAST WE WON. When I walk into the house through the garage and type in the code to re-arm the security system, I realize I'd be in a much worse mood if we'd lost.

The house is quiet, which is typical for 11:45 p.m. It's a school night. So Suki and the girls left the game around nine. She said they had a good time in a text earlier.

I'm fixing a plate of grilled chicken and roasted vegetables to heat up as a snack when I hear the beep of the security system. The French doors that lead from the family room to the patio and back yard are opened and I hear someone step in.

"Good boy, Darling," Suki croons. "You get a cookie."

The keypad beeps as she rearms the security system and then she comes around the corner.

"Hey," she says, smiling. "Congrats on the win."

"Thanks."

I take off my suit jacket and loosen my tie, watching her as she gets Darling a treat from the jar on the counter. He scarfs it out of her hand with a few snorts and then gives her a pleading look, wanting more.

She's still wearing my jersey. It's hard to be mad at her when she looks so good in it. The sleeves are rolled up and it hangs down to midthigh on her. It surprises me how much I like seeing her in it.

I've only had two girlfriends since going pro with hockey, and they both came to games and wore shirts and jerseys with my name on them. It was stuff they bought that any fan can buy, though. This is the first time I've seen a woman in one of my actual jerseys that I've also worn.

Suki is wearing it over black leggings, her hair up in a messy bun with little strands of hair around her face. She sits down to take off her snow boots.

"You should've told me about Naughty by Nature," I say, my tone a lot milder than it was in my head when I thought about this conversation on the drive home.

She sits up, her eyes widening. The boots are forgotten.

"What did you hear about it?"

The microwave beeps to tell me my food is done, but I ignore it. I walk over to the table she's sitting at, leaning against the island counter.

"Are the girls all asleep?" I ask softly.

"They were when I checked on them at ten thirty."

Her cheeks are slightly flushed from the cold. She was beautiful, all dressed up for the wedding, but tonight...there's something about seeing her so comfortable and casual in my jersey, looking so fresh and pretty, that makes me want to kiss her.

Even though I'm mad as hell at her. I don't get it.

"A hockey blogger looked into you when he heard we got married. He posted business paper-work for a company called Naughty by Nature and it says you're a co-owner."

She looks away, guilt in her expression.

"And you're pissed because of what the company sold."

"*Sold?* Past tense? No, Suki, I'm pissed because you didn't tell me about it. Because I had to find out in the locker room from my teammates seeing it online."

When she meets my gaze again, I see resolve in

her eyes. "It's not like I'm proud of it. It was my ex-boyfriend's business and he asked me to cosign on some loans and be listed as a co-owner. He told me it would give me legal protections to be a co-owner."

"Legal protections?" I shake my head. "And you believed him?"

"Obviously." She shrugs, her tone icy. "Then, when the company didn't do well, he left the country and now I'm responsible for all the debt."

I arch my brows, surprised a woman as savvy as Suki ended up in this situation.

"You should've told me."

She glares at me. "Did you tell me every secret from your past? Every mistake you've ever made?"

"No, but I'm...I guess, for lack of a better word, I'm the *employer* in this relationship. The one writing the check, not the one cashing it. I'm the one under constant public scrutiny because of my job. And if the company sold watches or something, it would be no big deal."

"Do you want out?"

I furrow my brow, confused. "Out of what?"

She holds up her hand and points at her ring. "This. You're the *employer*, so are you firing me?"

"Look, I didn't mean it like that."

"If you want out, it's fine."

That's the last fucking thing I need. A quickie

wedding followed by a quickie divorce or annulment less than a week late won't help the custody case.

"No, I don't want out. But we need to talk about this and anything else that could bite us in the ass. You're living under a spotlight now."

She nods, looking angry but also defeated.

"Is the company still open?"

"No. I never had anything to do with running it. When he left, I had to change the business address to my apartment so I could pay the bills and receive the inventory. I have a storage unit where I keep it all."

"How much debt do you have?"

She narrows her eyes. "That's none of your business. I'm current on the payments. That's all you need to know."

"Is there anything else that could hurt us if it came out? Like him selling his shit to minors or getting arrested?"

"Not that I know of, but he's a man, so he was probably hiding and lying more than I ever knew about."

Wow. Bitter, party of one. Suki seems to have decided to blame my entire gender for what her douchebag ex did.

I unbutton my dress shirt, suddenly tired. I just want to eat and go to bed. The rest of this conversation can wait.

"Are we done?" she asks, her tone curt.

"Yeah."

She scoops Darling up from the floor and walks away without another word.

I eat my food in silence, wishing I'd gone for the postgame snack I really wanted. Lucky Charms cereal.

Suki

"AUNT ROSIE, this is Darling. Isn't he handsome?"

Hallie walks him into the kitchen on his leash, and he immediately heads for the pantry, tugging the leash taut.

"He's the handsomest pig I've ever seen," Rosie says. "I can't wait to get to know him better."

"Can he have a snack?" Hallie looks at me.

"A little one. Maybe some crackers. He's gaining weight so quickly; we need to keep the sugary snacks down."

Rosie laughs. "How big is he going to get?"

"We don't know. He's a micro pig, but he's growing like crazy."

Carter walks into the room, a packed overnight bag in each hand. "Hey, Aunt Rosie."

He sets the bags down and walks over to hug her.

"You look good," she says warmly as she embraces him. "And I just love Darling. What a great idea that was."

Carter frowns. "I'm not so sure about that. He pissed on my shoes again."

"He's still a baby." Hallie gives him a serious look as Darling scarfs Goldfish out of her hand. "You can't get mad at a baby."

"Maybe he needs a diaper then," Carter quips, making Hallie laugh.

"Suki left me instructions for him," Rosie says. "And did you say he sleeps in bed with the girls?"

"He does, but he always ends up in Charlotte's bed because she keeps snacks under her bed for him."

"What?" Hallie's jaw drops. "She said he just loves her the most."

Carter growls with disapproval. "I told Charlotte to quit doing that."

"Never mind for now," Rosie says. "You two are already getting too short of a honeymoon. You need to get out of here immediately."

I can't say I'm looking forward to a weekend alone with Carter in Ann Arbor, Michigan, but it'll be nice to sleep in and not have to wake up early to take Darling out.

"There's mostaccioli in the fridge you can use for dinner tonight if you want to," I tell Rosie. "I left instructions on a note and taped it to the top. And Olivia's present for the birthday party tomorrow is on the dining table. You're picking up her friend Kate at twelve forty-five and dropping both girls off at the party. Kate's address and the party address are on the paper I left. Kate's mom will bring Olivia home after the party."

Rosie gives me a warm smile. "I like the way you do things, Suki. Thank you for all your work making this weekend easier for me."

She looks like she's in her late fifties, her hair styled in a short, feathered silver bob. I liked her immediately when we met.

"No problem at all."

Hallie runs over and throws her arms around my waist. "I'll miss you."

I hug her back, bending to kiss the top of her head. "I'll miss you, too. But I know you guys will have the best time with Aunt Rosie."

Rosie gives Carter a pointed look. "What do you do around this house other than look good and carry the bags to the car?"

"He colors with me," Hallie says, hugging him. "And he makes good popcorn."

"Well, good."

Carter gives me a questioning look. "You ready?"

"Yeah."

"Where are Olivia and Charlotte?" Rosie asks.

"In their rooms. I said goodbye to them already."

"I better go do that," Carter says.

Hallie gently tugs Darling's leash, bringing him closer to me.

"Darling wants a kiss and hug."

I laugh. "How about ear scratches and belly rubs?"

I love on Darling while Carter is gone, and he's back in the kitchen within two minutes. I'm sure he literally just said "bye" to both girls. But at least he said something, I guess.

Things have been tense between us since our conversation about the business. I liked it better when he didn't know a single one of my weaknesses or past mistakes. Now I feel exposed, and I don't like it.

Carter puts our bags in the back of his Lincoln Navigator and we start the drive in silence for the first fifteen minutes.

"If you want some of the five hundred thousand dollars now, I can do that," he says out of nowhere.

"However much you owe on those loans, there's no reason to rack up another year of interest."

It's a nice offer. I fight my urge to tell him to drop the subject. Simply because it makes me so uncomfortable to talk about anything related to how stupid it was of me to trust Tyler so much.

"That would be nice."

"Would three hundred be enough?"

I decide to bite the bullet and be honest with him. If online sleuths keep sleuthing, it'll only be a matter of time before it's public record anyway.

"Two hundred would be enough. I owe just over a hundred and eighty thousand."

He nods, a cringe flickering across his face. "I'll take care of it Monday. My accountant will need your account information for a wire transfer."

"Thank you."

He sighs softly. "I shouldn't have gotten so mad about it."

"I get it. You're paying me a lot of money for this arrangement. I never imagined anyone would dig into my past like that."

"I was a dick about it, Suki. I'm used to the way I communicate with my teammates and that's not how I should be communicating with you and the girls."

I've never seen Carter be contrite. It's endearing,

him admitting he was a dick, his half scowl in place and his massive hand wrapped around the steering wheel.

"It's okay." I glance over at him. "So, where are we going in Ann Arbor?"

"I booked us an Airbnb just outside the city on a lake. It's cold as shit there, so I got a place with fireplaces. There's a chef coming to make us dinner there tonight and I figured we can go out tomorrow night."

"That sounds nice."

"I've always liked Ann Arbor."

"Did you used to go there with the archaeologist?"

He shakes his head. "Kaia lived in New York, so we only saw each other two or three times a month. She'd fly in for weekends when I had home games. When we spent more time together during my offseason, that was when we argued the most."

I can't help being nosy; I'm dying of curiosity about his relationship with her. "Were the arguments her fault or yours?"

A smile plays on his lips. "Probably sixty percent me and forty percent her. She liked the New York nightlife a lot, you know? Wanted to take me to all these dinner parties with her friends and colleagues, and it just wasn't my jam. And she just wanted more out of the relationship than I did."

"How long were you guys together?"

"Almost two years. She gave me an ultimatum that if we weren't engaged after two years, she was out."

"And she didn't wait the full two years?"

He shrugs. "I told her it wasn't happening."

"Do you ever second-guess your decision?"

"No. I talked to Rachel about it a lot. She thought Kaia was too controlling and in too much of a hurry to have a husband with money."

He touches the screen in his car, glancing at me. "What kind of music do you like?"

"Mostly jazz."

He lowers his brows. "Really?"

"Hell no. I like Taylor Swift, Lizzo, Ed Sheeran, Gracie Abrams. How about you?"

"I listen to a lot of Eminem, Post Malone, old rock. Got lots of Metallica on my pregame playlist right now."

"Hmm." I smile. "I'm not sure we have much overlap."

"The girls made me become a Swiftie. It's all we listen to in the car."

"Same." I take off my seat belt and lean forward to slide out of my coat. "There are mornings where we just sing the entire drive to school instead of talking."

He selects a Taylor Swift playlist from his screen and turns the volume down so we can hear it but still talk.

"I spilled my guts about my ex, so what's the story with yours? Other than him being a massive douchebag?"

Discomfort stabs me in the gut, but I swallow it. "I was an idiot who trusted a man I'd only been with for ten months. He meant more to me than I meant to him and I got burned. That's about it."

"Did he have a job when you met him?"

"He worked for a venture capital firm. He made good money but lost it all by going all in on his business idea."

"It sucks that he took you down with him."

I shrug and look away. "It was my own fault. There's a reason why I didn't tell my family and friends about cosigning those loans. I knew it was dumb, but I thought we were in love."

"Do you still love him?"

I'm caught so off guard by the question that my laugh comes out as a little snort. "Absolutely not. I'd punch him in the dick if I saw him on the street."

"If we see him in Ann Arbor, I'll give you an

assist. I'll hold on to him so you can wind up hard for that punch. Maybe follow up with a nice kick."

"I appreciate it."

It's the first time anything related to Tyler has amused me. Usually I just feel bitter and angry.

I take out my list of stuff about me and read it, Carter learning that I love standing outside when it's snowing and reading sci-fi romance novels and I hate peas.

When he passes me his list, it's full of little details about him that make me smile.

"Your top three favorite foods are Cinnamon Toast Crunch, Cocoa Puffs and Honeycomb? I thought those were for the girls."

"I mean, they eat some, too. But I can take down about half a box of cereal on a cheat day."

"Okay, so cereal is just a treat for you?"

"Unfortunately. It's not that I love grilled chicken that much; it's just that it's good for me and I make a living with my body."

"That sounds dirty."

He grins. "Yeah, it does."

We talk for the entire drive to our destination, and the tension between us from last night is forgotten. When Carter pulls up to a massive lakefront home with a modern design, I gape at him.

"Here? Is this like a bed-and-breakfast with tons

of rooms?"

He makes a face. "Fuck no. This whole place is ours for the weekend."

"No way! This is beautiful."

"Can't take my fake wife to Motel 6 for our fake honeymoon, can I?"

"I mean, you could. But I'm glad you went a different direction."

When we walk into the sprawling home, I'm like an awestruck kid in a candy store. The main area is an open two stories with a gorgeous stone fireplace surround and a modern stainless kitchen. The entire back wall of the home is made of windows to maximize views of the sparkling water.

"You can pick your room first," Carter says as he sets both our bags down.

Separate bedrooms. What a relief. I don't have to smell his soap on my bedsheets or worry about accidentally rolling into him for the next two nights.

It *should* be a relief. But it's kind of not.

———

"WHAT IS HE DOING?" I mumble to myself as Carter carries a huge satin silver pothos plant out of the Ann Arbor store we were just browsing in.

The boutique is next door to the restaurant

where we had a late Saturday breakfast and I saw the beautiful plant behind the register. I admired it and told Carter a plant like that would easily go for several hundred dollars.

"Did you steal that?" I say when he opens the door to the back seat and sets the plant on the floor.

He scoffs. "No, I didn't steal it. I bought it."

We were on our way out to the car when he said he needed to run back in and use the bathroom. Clearly, he was actually going back for the plant.

"You bought it?" I ask as he gets into the driver's seat.

"You wanted it, right?"

It takes me a couple of seconds to respond. "Yes, I love it. But it wasn't for sale."

"I asked the store owner how much she wanted for it, so it was for sale."

My stomach does a full somersault. Plants are my love language. My apartment is a mini jungle.

"Thank you."

The emotion in my voice gives away how unusual it is for me to get a thoughtful gift from a man. Tyler once took a fifty from his wallet and gave it to me on my birthday, saying he hadn't had time to shop for anything.

"Yeah, no problem," Carter says, not even looking at me.

I smile to myself. He's like this with the girls, too. He accepts tenderness and affection about as well as a grizzly bear would.

Yesterday, I lounged around the house, enjoying the views and reading. Carter went for a long run, and a chef came and made us an amazing dinner of steak, scalloped potatoes, roasted vegetables and flan.

We talked and laughed like old friends, watching a movie before I went to bed in a room where I had a king-size bed all to myself.

This morning, Carter was already at the kitchen table when I came in, freshly showered and having a cup of coffee, the Henrietta Lacks book in hand.

"Want to go throw some axes?" he asks.

"Sure. Do you have some in the back seat we can just hurl out the car windows?"

He smiles. "I thought we'd do something more organized. There's a local place."

It only takes us ten minutes to get there, and when we do, the guy working behind the counter does a double take when he sees Carter.

"Stanton...you're Carter Stanton. From the Crush."

"Yeah." Carter shakes his hand and the guy asks for a selfie with him.

Then we're assigned a lane and given some basic

instructions on axe throwing. Of course, Carter is a natural, getting the axe to stick exactly where he wants it almost every time.

I can barely even get it to reach the target, let alone hit it.

"I'm hopeless," I grumble when yet another axe lands on the ground.

"Here." Carter grabs an axe and comes over, standing behind me.

He's solid and warm, my ears on the same level as his broad shoulders. His flannel has the scent of his light leather and pine cologne. Nervousness coils low in my belly as he puts the axe in my hand, covering my hands with his own.

"Back more." His voice is a soft caress on my ear, making me shiver.

He moves one of his hands to my stomach, placing a flat palm there as he says, "Use your core."

I'm going to melt. Every nerve ending in my body is firing and heat is flooding me. Carter is more man than every guy I've ever been with added together. And then multiplied by ten.

"Ready?"

I nod, not trusting my voice. He does most of the work for me, and the axe lands left of center, but at least it's on the target.

"Nice job." He puts a palm on my lower back as

he steps away.

What happened to my plan to never be with another man again? If Carter asked me to go have sex in his car right now, I don't think I could say no.

It's my traitorous body overruling my good sense. I can't let myself fall for another man.

"I'm taking a break," I say, walking over to our table and sitting down.

I watch him throw axes for another hour, and then we walk to a local bookstore and a few more boutiques. We have dinner at a local microbrewery, and even several hours later, I'm still feeling pulled toward Carter.

I want to be close enough to smell him and feel his solid body against my much softer one. I want to see if I can possibly undo him the way he's unknowingly doing to me.

I trust my instincts, though, and instead of watching another movie with him, I go to my room to read.

I fell in love with a fake in Tyler and got burned. Carter has been completely transparent about our relationship being fake. Not real. All for show.

Stick to the plan, Suki. One year. For the girls. And the money.

Then, I can start over and make all my decisions based only on what's best for me.

CHAPTER TWELVE

Suki

"THIS DUCK IS GOING to be fabulous," Harry promises as he chops fresh spices on a wooden cutting board. "I always sell out of this early at the restaurant."

I look up from the potatoes I'm peeking at and blow him a kiss. "I owe you for this."

He waves a hand dismissively. "I'm happy to be here. You know my family only talks about sports and politics on holidays. And they serve that canned cranberry gel garbage."

"I love you, but that stuff is delicious."

He cringes dramatically. "It's not even food. Wait until you try my cranberry orange relish. We're serving it on baked Brie."

I don't remind him that I've tried his relish already. I'm just not a fancy food girl. Give me some old-school Kraft macaroni and cheese any day.

Mara and Dex are spending Thanksgiving with their families. They're coming over tomorrow night to play games, though--a tradition we started three years ago.

Darling waddles into the kitchen and comes over to me, snorting as he sniffs the ground for scraps. When he finds nothing, he looks up at me with a pleading expression.

"That baby is hungry," Harry says.

"He wants Goldfish," Olivia says from the other side of the kitchen, where she's peeling and slicing apples.

"He ate a Costco-sized box in two days," I say. "Plus his regular diet the vet wants us feeding him."

"Come here, Darling." Harry bends down, offering Darling a Ritz cracker with seafood dip.

Darling inhales it, then nuzzles against Harry in thanks.

"Uncle Harry could never say no to you," Harry croons. "You're just a big sweetheart."

That *sweetheart* dragged a bunch of hay into our bed a few days ago and I had to wash the sheets and blankets to get rid of all the little shards. He also shredded several pairs of Carter's underwear, which the girls found hilarious.

But he's doing well with house-training. I give him pieces of granola bars when he potties outside and he caught on pretty quickly. That pig would dance a jig if he thought he could get food for it.

"Hey, Harry." Carter walks into the kitchen with a smile and my heart skips a beat.

He goes over to Harry, hugs him and thanks him for helping. I don't know if my heart is reacting to the way he looks in his navy Brooks Brothers sweater with a dress shirt beneath it or to his greeting of Harry.

I really like how warm Carter is to my friends. He makes sure they feel welcome when they're over.

"You look great," Harry tells Carter. "I feel under-dressed."

"We're all underdressed compared to him," I say, gesturing at my ripped jeans and my T-shirt, which has a big slice of pumpkin pie covered with whipped cream and says, 'It's me, pie. I'm the problem it's me.'

"Well, I'm meeting my in-laws for the first time," Carter says. "I figured I should look decent."

My stomach rolls with dread. I just texted my family this morning to tell them that the "boyfriend" I invited them to meet today is actually my husband.

My phone is currently face down on the dresser in the bedroom because managing the incoming texts would be a full-time job.

I check the clock on the wall. Based on the drive time from their home in Chicago, if my parents got in the car as soon as I sent the text, they could be arriving any minute. My brothers Nate and Sean are riding here with them, and Jack is coming this evening; he and his girlfriend driving from Philadelphia.

"So...my family hasn't known about our marriage for long," I say casually.

"What does that mean?" Carter asks. "How long is *not long*?"

I keep my gaze on the potatoes, knowing I should have told them sooner. I just knew how it would go. Invited for a holiday or not, my family would have come running here in reaction to the news that I got married to a man I haven't even known for three months and they weren't invited.

"I told them this morning." I look at Harry immediately. "What should I do with the potatoes when I'm done peeling them?"

Harry is staring at me, open-mouthed.

"This morning?" Carter demands loudly. "Are you fucking kidding me, Suki?"

"It'll be fine," I lie. "I just wanted to wait as long as

possible because I knew they'd be...opinionated about not getting invited to the wedding."

He glares at me. "Should I get my pads on? Is this going to get ugly?"

Charlotte and Hallie come into the kitchen with Charlotte saying, "Darling, let's get your Thanksgiving sweater on!"

The sweater is cute as hell. Clothes made for bulldogs fit Darling well, and this sweater is plaid with fall colors. He rolls onto his back for belly rubs and I try to exit the conversation with Carter by helping the girls put the sweater on him.

"Suki."

Carter's beside us now, not letting me off that easy. I look up at him, trying to figure out what to say when the doorbell rings.

"I'll get it!" Hallie runs off, Darling trotting behind her.

Charlotte looks between the two of us, reading the situation well and leaving, too. I stand up and take Carter's hand.

"Let me handle it. I promise it'll be okay."

He looks over his shoulder, making sure Olivia is gone, too. "They have to think we're madly in love. If they don't, they're going to hate me for asking you to marry me so fast."

"I can--we can convince them. I think."

"Where is this guy?"

I close my eyes as I hear my stepdad's deep voice. Tony has always been more like a dad to me than a stepdad since I was a baby when my dad passed away and my mom married Tony three years after that.

Carter gives my hand a little squeeze and releases it, turning toward the family room just as my dad walks into the kitchen.

"Mr. Brennan, it's great to meet you, sir." Carter walks over to him and extends his hand. "I'm Carter Stanton."

Dad ignores his hand, looking at me with an expression that's a mix of anger and hurt.

"What is this, Suki? You married this man we've never even met? Is this a joke?"

My mom is right behind him, and when she sees Carter's outstretched hand, she comes to the rescue.

"Tony." She nods at Carter's hand.

Dad begrudgingly reaches out and shakes Carter's hand. Carter extends his hand to my mom next.

"Mrs. Brennan, I'm glad to finally meet you, ma'am. Thanks for making the trip to spend Thanksgiving with us."

She shakes his hand and smiles. "I'm Reina and

he's Tony. Thank you for having us. We're excited to meet your nieces and spend some time with all of you." She takes my dad's arm and looks up at him. "Aren't we, Tony?"

"Yes," my dad grates out, his eyes narrowed. "Really excited."

I go over to my parents, hugging my mom tightly.

"Thank you, I love you," I whisper in her ear.

Then I hug my dad, who softens. His expression is filled with love when he stands back and looks at me.

"I expected to get a visit from any man who wanted to marry my little girl. I thought I'd walk you down the aisle. Why did you have to rush things?"

I open my mouth to respond, but I can't think of an answer. Carter jumps in.

"It was my fault, Mr. Brennan. Suki and I are so in love I just couldn't wait another day to marry her. And you're right. I should have asked your permission."

Dad scowls at him. "You wouldn't have gotten it. I don't even know you."

"How about some appetizers?" Harry says brightly. "I thought I'd put some things out on the buffet in the dining room."

"It smells wonderful in here," my mom says.

She grabs my dad's arm and practically drags him from the kitchen. I look through the open doorway and see my brothers, Nate and Sean. Nate is bent down petting Darling and Sean is talking to Charlotte.

I don't get to see my brothers enough. Nate is a firefighter in Des Moines and Sean is a middle school social studies teacher in Minneapolis.

Carter and I go into the family room together to greet them. They both hug us and congratulate us, but I can see my brothers not so secretly sizing Carter up.

"That was a nice six-hour trip listening to Dad rant nonstop," Nate says wryly.

"Can you blame him?" Sean gives me a questioning look. "That was a pretty huge bombshell for a text."

Carter slides his arm around my waist, pulling me closer. "It's my fault we didn't handle things better. I'll do my best to make it up to all of you."

"I'll never not see Suki as my kid sister," Sean says. "It's hard to imagine her as someone's wife."

"She's amazing." Carter gives me a loving gaze so convincing it makes my heart pound. "She's the most nurturing, funny, kindhearted woman I've ever known."

"I already like you better than her last boyfriend," Sean says. "Fancy job or not, he was a jackass."

"No shit," Sean agrees. He looks over at Hallie. "Sorry."

"They're used to it," Carter says. "What can I get you guys to drink?"

I return to the kitchen to help Harry with the cooking, trying to keep an eye on things in the family room. My parents are talking to the girls and Carter is sticking close to my brothers.

"Mara's going to be so bummed she missed this one," Harry says lightly, passing me a glass of wine he just poured me.

I sigh wearily. "Isn't it funny how your parents can take you from feeling like a fully functioning adult to feeling like a kid who needs to go stand in the corner?"

"We'll look back and laugh at this one day," he assures me.

Carter's teammate Bash arrives next, lightening the mood since he's unaware of the tension. Our housekeeper Andrea and her son Drew also arrive. They don't have any family here, so I invited them to spend the day with us.

By the time we get the meal on the table, I'm optimistic that my dad's bad mood has passed.

Carter takes my hand beneath the table, probably hoping my family will see him being affectionate.

He releases it quickly, though, standing up with his water goblet in hand.

"Hey guys, just a quick toast." Everyone quiets and looks at him. "We're so glad all of you could be here with us today. Thank you to Harry and my beautiful wife for preparing this meal, it looks incredible." He meets my gaze, my heart still fluttering from the *beautiful wife* thing. "Suki, anyone who's lucky enough to be around you is better for it. I'll keep spending every day trying to make you half as happy as you make me."

Glasses clink, but my glass just stays frozen in the air as Carter sits down, still looking at me. He leans over and gives me a quick kiss, leaving me even more dazed.

This whole fake relationship thing is playing with my head. I remind myself I'm only Carter's "beautiful wife" to help him get custody of the girls.

"So Carter, how many times have you been married?" my dad asks, his tone less than friendly.

"Just this time."

"Did you get my daughter pregnant?"

"Dad!" I snap, mortified.

"Mrs. Brennan, your olive dip is absolutely

divine," Harry says smoothly. "I'd love to get the recipe from you."

Carter puts a hand on my knee beneath the table, silently reassuring me. I knew this day wouldn't be perfect, but I thought my dad had more tact than this. Asking if I'm pregnant at the Thanksgiving table? My mom is going to give him hell later.

"Want some turkey, Darling?" Charlotte leans over to haul the twenty-five-plus pound pig onto her lap.

Carter frowns. "Hey, Char, I don't--"

Darling gets his front two feet onto the table, scrambling out of Charlotte's hold. It feels like I'm in slow motion as I lunge at him. He tramples my beautiful floral centerpieces on his way down the dining table, knocking over water goblets and stepping in the gravy.

He's going for the giant bowl of garlic mashed potatoes at the end of the table, and when he gets there, he dives in with his whole face, snorting as he inhales the food.

Everyone scoots their chairs back from the table, watching Darling in stunned silence. I exchange a horrified look with Harry.

Carter goes to that end of the table and wraps his arms around Darling's midsection, picking him up and carrying him away. Darling looks back at all of us, his snout covered with mashed potatoes. It almost looks like he's smiling.

Hallie is the first to laugh. The other two girls look at me, trying to decide if it's okay to laugh. When I look at Harry, he's smiling.

"I'll go see what else we can whip up," he says, getting up from the table.

Charlotte gives me a remorseful look. "I'm sorry, Suki. That was my fault."

I laugh because what else can I do? Once my family sees me laughing, they join in. Other than my dad, who still looks pissed off.

"Girls, why don't we work together and get this mess cleaned up?" Sean says, rising from his chair.

When Carter comes into the kitchen a few minutes later, he's taken his sweater off and rolled up the sleeves of his dress shirt. He sees me holding a pan of sweet potato casserole with a pig footprint in it and takes it, moving it onto the island.

"Darling is in our shower," he says. "I put some blankets in there. Hopefully he won't ruin anything."

Bash comes up and puts a hand on my shoulder and a hand on Carter's. "I wasn't hungry anyway. You want me to see if I can find an open carryout place?"

Carter nods. "That'd be good, thanks."

Bash walks away and I step closer to Carter, whispering, "I'm sorry about my dad."

He opens his arms and wraps me in a hug, kissing the top of my head. "We'll get through it."

Fake relationship. Not his real feelings. I have to remind myself yet again because he smells really good and I didn't realize just how much I needed a hug right now.

CHAPTER THIRTEEN

Suki

FOUR WEEKS LATER

"So while both the Yeti and the Stanley are both excellent cups for hot and cold drinks, I believe the clear winner after my tests is the Yeti."

Dex grins widely and claps as Olivia finishes practicing the speech he helped her write and coached her on performing. Mara, Harry and I all join in on the applause.

Olivia meets my gaze and smiles. In just a few days, Dex took her from overwhelmed and nervous to poised and confident.

"I'll be tossing my Stanley when I get home," Dex

says proudly. "Can you believe this girl? She needs to be on the speech team."

"That was amazing," I tell Olivia, hugging her. "You'll have to do it again for Carter."

It's Christmas Eve, and my friends have come over to hang out with me and the girls while Carter does some last-minute shopping. Harry brought home-made cinnamon rolls, so we're all sugared up. Darling is curled up, sleeping at Harry's feet like he knows who made the sticky-sweet treat he loved so much.

"Are you guys ready to make some gingerbread houses?" I ask.

The girls have been excited about this for days, so they're the first to arrive in the dining room and sit down.

I tried to plan a fun day since this is their first Christmas without their mom. This afternoon we're going to a family skate at Carter's team arena, then to a downtown Christmas market.

I already have a lasagna in the refrigerator for dinner and we're making ice cream sundaes and watching Christmas movies after that.

I'm gathering the last of the gingerbread supplies in the kitchen when Mara touches my arm.

"Hey, remember that professor I had a thing for last year?"

I scoff. "Remember? You talked about Professor Lumberjack constantly and texted me all your stalker research about him from social media. I feel like his close personal friend."

"A yes would suffice."

I shake my head, amused. "Yes, I remember."

"Well, the other night, wine gave me the balls to message him. I told him I passed the bar and would love to celebrate over drinks sometime." She grabs my arm, biting her lip as she grins. "He said yes. He fucking said yes. Professor Lumberjack is going to be balls deep in me within a week."

"Or...he just wants to catch up with a former student."

"Psst. He's gonna be catching my ankles and putting them over those big-ass shoulders, girl. Sweet baby Jesus, this is my Christmas miracle. I just know he's gonna have a big"--she glances toward the dining room--"*brain*. God, I hope he leaves his glasses on."

"I'm happy for you. Now let's go decorate gingerbread houses."

"Mine's going to be a brothel. A little candy den of sin where gingerbread men go to wreck slutty little gingerbread women."

"Okay, one track mind. You need to go get some

supplies from my storage bay before you start air humping."

"That's fair."

Dex and Harry are helping the girls use frosting to attach the walls and roofs to their houses when Mara and I walk into the room. I've just sat down to start working on mine when Carter comes in.

"Hey," he says, his gaze meeting mine when he walks into the room.

The past month we've gotten into a nice routine. He's been busy with hockey, but on his off days, he always hangs out with us. He's reading Hallie Harry Potter and teaching Charlotte how to play hockey.

"Hey, I set up stuff for you if you want to make a gingerbread house," I say.

"Make one, Uncle Carter," Hallie says. "Please?"

"I'll see what I can do."

He sits down next to Hallie and I feel his eyes on me. I blew my hair out this morning and did a full face of makeup instead of my usual messy bun, foundation and mascara. I'm wearing a black V-neck shirt that's lower cut than I realized until I put it on, with jeans and ballet flats.

Darling comes into the room, nose to the ground as he snorts and looks for something to root around in. I've had to move all my beloved houseplants out of his reach because he can't resist rooting in the dirt.

"What the hell?" Mara blurts. "I was just here two weeks ago and he's gotten so much bigger."

Darling weighs almost sixty pounds now. He eats everything in sight but is very good-natured and loves snuggling with the girls.

"Yeah…" I look at Carter. "I found out at our last vet visit that Darling isn't actually a micro pig," I say. "He's just a regular old hog."

Mara's jaw drops. "Seriously? How big is he going to get?"

I send soothing vibes Carter's way before I answer. "Somewhere between two hundred fifty and five hundred pounds."

He sets down the tube of frosting he's holding, closing his eyes and pinching the bridge of his nose. I already told him this, but it seems to be causing him a fresh wave of aggravation.

"Five hundred pounds!" Olivia cries. "We won't be able to hold him anymore."

"Did the breeder misrepresent him?" Dex asks Carter.

"I'm going to ask my friend Leo. He's the one who set it up for us."

"We're still keeping him, right?" Charlotte asks, her tone worried.

Carter blows out a breath. "We can't have a five-hundred-pound farm hog in the house, Char."

"No!" Hallie cries, tears filling her eyes. "I love him!"

"He might only be two fifty," Olivia says hopefully.

I lock eyes with Carter and say, "We'll make it work."

"Does that mean we don't have to get rid of him?" Charlotte asks.

I silently tell Carter that he can either make the right decision now or after we argue privately, but we aren't getting rid of the girls' beloved pet, and I don't want them worrying about it on Christmas Eve.

He shakes his head. "Fine. He can just eat all the carpet in the house, I guess."

"Carpet's over," Dex says lightly. "Put in hardwood."

"That's what she said," Mara says under her breath.

Everyone but Hallie and Carter laughs. When I glance at Carter a few seconds later, I swear I see heat in his gaze. Like he's telling me he just gave me my way and now he's going to have his.

I exhale slowly, focusing on building my ginger-bread house. It was probably just my overactive imagination. Lots of women would kill to be his plaything, many of them much sexier and more alluring than I am.

———

HALLIE SQUEALS with excitement as Carter spins on his skates, glancing over his shoulder and skating backward while holding her.

The Crush family skate is a bigger event than I realized. The team has Santa and some elves in a suite, passing out gifts and listening to wish lists. There's a full buffet and a lavish hot cocoa bar with candy, marshmallows and other toppings layered on tiered trays. The whole arena is decked in fresh garland and holiday decor.

Next to me, Charlotte's hand slips out of mine as her feet slide out from beneath her and she lands on her butt for at least the tenth time.

"I think I'm done," she says, looking defeated.

"No, that was on me. I should have been holding your hand tighter."

She cringes as she gets up, looking adorable in her purple knit beanie and purple vest.

"It's hot chocolate time," she says.

"I could go for some hot chocolate."

Olivia left us as soon as we got onto the ice,

heading straight for the friends she's made with other kids with family on the team.

Charlotte and I are almost to the swinging doors leading off the ice when Carter slides to a quick stop next to us, throwing up ice.

"Show-off," Charlotte says, rolling her eyes.

He grins and sets Hallie down, then looks at me and says, "Your turn."

My brows shoot up. "My turn? For what?"

He takes one of my gloved hands. "To skate with me."

"Yeah, no. I can't keep up."

"We're not in a race. I just want to take my wife for a few turns around the rink."

I'm his wife. The oval solitaire ring on my finger confirms it. Still, my heart skips every time he calls me that. There's something about hearing him say it that makes me a little giddy.

"I'll take Halls to get hot chocolate," Charlotte says, reaching for her sister's hand.

"Thanks," I say.

Carter holds both of my hands, smoothly spinning into a backward skating position once again.

"Having fun?" he asks.

"Yeah."

"You've ice-skated before."

"Five years of figure skating lessons. I once did a

routine to "Last Friday Night" by Katy Perry and won second place."

"Wow. Why am I just hearing about this accomplishment?"

I shrug. "I didn't want to intimidate you."

"We can do a lift if you want."

I laugh. "I didn't make it that far."

He closes some of the space between us, moving our hands out to the side, his expression soft as he says. "Thanks for everything you're doing to make this Christmas good for the girls."

"I love doing it."

"You've been their rock. Mine, too."

I swallow hard, taken aback by the compliment. Carter is usually aloof and sometimes downright gruff. But on those occasions when he says something sweet, he knocks it out of the park every time.

"Well...I'm glad to be."

I hold back a cringe over my awkwardness. Every time we're alone, I worry I'll let slip that I want him. A lot. I've stopped trying to make myself not want him because it's impossible. As long as I don't act on it, it won't be a problem.

He releases my hands and comes even closer, putting his hands on my waist as he glances over his shoulder.

"Team photographer is taking pictures of us," he murmurs.

Of course. Why else would he be looking at me like that? His expression is a mix of tenderness and happiness.

"Watch it, Stanton," one of his teammates jokes as he skates past us. "I'm trying to smoke some six-year-olds and you're in my way."

Carter shakes his head, something over my shoulder catching his eye. He scowls.

"Who's that boy Olivia's smiling at?"

I turn to see where he's looking. "Oh, I bet that's Jake. She mentioned him."

"Really." He says it angrily. "He looks about fifteen, and whose kid is he? I don't know him."

"We can ask her later."

"Or now."

"Carter..."

"What? If he asks for her number, I'll board the little fucker."

I give him a look. "Don't embarrass her. She's just trying to fit in with the other kids. Let's just enjoy Christmas Eve."

He looks from Olivia to me. "Fine. But we're talking to her later."

"Not later tonight, though. Because it's Christmas. Fucking. Eve."

"Okay, fine."

A woman in a Crush hoodie with a camera in hand skates toward us.

"Carter, can you get your whole family onto the ice for a photo?"

"Sure." He looks at me. "You want to get Charlotte and Hallie?"

I smile. "No, I'll get Liv. *You* get Charlotte and Hallie."

He nods, not looking happy about it.

When the photographer gets us all together and poses us in the middle of the rink for a photo, I get that same feeling I had when the wedding photographer was taking photos. Like looking at this picture will hurt someday.

Only this time, I know it'll hurt worse. The closer I get to Carter and the girls, the harder it is to know the clock is ticking on our little family.

Only he and I know that our first Christmas together is also our last. Unless I can somehow convince him to keep me on as his nanny after our marriage ends.

I've already started thinking about it. It would be awkward at first, but we could make it work. I planned to start over after the year, but leaving the girls would break my heart.

Seeing him with another woman would do the

same thing, though. Could I go back to just being his nanny while he dates women like Kaia, maybe even marrying one someday?

I don't know. Right now, none of the options seem great.

CHAPTER FOURTEEN

Carter

"UNCLE CARTER."

I try to brush away the tickle of something near my earlobe. There's a giggle.

"Uncle Carter, it's Christmas."

I open my eyes and see the outline of Hallie sitting next to me in bed. When I sit up, I see Darling lying in the center of the bed, snoring.

"Suki said to let you sleep until the sun comes up. I didn't wake you up, did I?"

"What time is it?"

Suki's side of the bed is empty. I pick up my phone from the nightstand and check the screen. It's 4:11 a.m.

Fuck me, it's early. But Hallie is low-key bouncing with excitement. There's no way she's going back to bed.

"Okay, are we opening presents now?" I ask.

"Yes! I'll go get Charlotte and Olivia."

She races from the room and I go to the bathroom. I'm a little more awake after splashing water on my face and brushing my teeth.

I leave Darling to sleep and head downstairs, the lights from the tree creating a soft glow in the family room. Suki is kneeling in front of the tree, doing something with a gift.

The three stockings hanging from the mantle are all filled and there are gifts stacked on gifts beneath and around the tree. I stop and take it all in, a pang of guilt hitting me in the gut.

I should have helped with all of this. I watched SportsCenter in the bedroom until I fell asleep.

"Merry Christmas." Suki looks up at me and smiles, then stands up.

She's not even mad. I didn't help her with any of this and she's not even mad about it.

"Merry Christmas. It looks incredible in here."

"Thanks. Did Hallie wake you up?"

"Officially, no."

She laughs softly. "She's really excited."

Footsteps pound on the stairs and I turn to see all

three girls racing down. I switch on a light and walk over to sit down on the couch.

"It's clothes!" Olivia says as she shakes a box.

All three girls are dressed in Grinch pajamas that Suki picked out, and she's wearing matching ones. Charlotte's hair is freshly pink after a trip to Suki's hairstylist the other day. Olivia is getting tall and looking more like her mom.

I wish Rachel could see her daughters and know they're doing okay. Better than okay. They're good. They'll never stop missing her, but they smile more and cry a lot less than they did when they first moved in.

That's because of Suki. She's glowing with happiness as she watches them. She's beautiful and sharp and funny, but the way she nurtures all of us is every bit as attractive to me as the other things, if not more.

She laughs at something Charlotte says and I smile just looking at her. I didn't plan on developing feelings for her, but I have. When I'm on the road and I lie down in a hotel bed, I wish she was there. I fantasize about her, even when she is beside me in bed.

I thought I was just sex-deprived at first, but the truth is, I don't want any other woman. Suki wears my jersey to games and has my ring on her finger.

She's my wife. That's supposed to terrify me, but it doesn't.

Is it so wrong to want to bang your own wife into next week and not want anyone else? Feels pretty damn good to me, but I don't know if she'd agree.

"The first gift is for Suki, and then you can go crazy and open your stuff, girls."

I walk over to the big wood cabinet thing the interior designer said would "anchor the entire room", whatever that means. I stashed a little box in here yesterday and I take it out.

"Carter," Suki says the moment she sees the little blue box with a white ribbon. "That's from Tiffany."

Her tone is warning me like I don't know where I bought the gift. I wink and pass it to her.

"Just open it, Suki."

"Who's Tiffany?" Hallie asks.

"It's a store," I say.

"A very expensive store," Suki says softly.

She slides the ribbon from the box, my blood pressure kicking up a notch. I hope this is a good idea. My gut tells me it is. My sister always told me I'm good at picking out thoughtful gifts.

"Oh, Carter." Suki looks from the contents of the box to me, her eyes flooded with emotion.

"What is it?" Olivia asks, beaming with excitement.

"It's the most beautiful necklace I've ever seen. It's a small vine of leaves covered with diamonds."

"A plant Darling can't eat," I explain.

Suki passes the box to Charlotte and the girls all crowd around it. She gets up from her seat on the floor and comes over to me, putting her arms around my neck in a hug.

"Thank you," she says softly. "I love it so much."

I hold her close, wishing for more than a hug. I've never been great at communicating about feelings. That's an understatement--I'm shit at it. Actions, though, I'm pretty good at.

"Put it on, Suki," Charlotte says.

Suki grins and goes over to the girls, Charlotte helping her get the necklace out of the box and put it on. It takes her a couple of minutes to get the clasp fastened, but Olivia doesn't jump her about it.

Rachel would be proud of her daughters right now. They aren't thinking about their gifts. They know Suki deserves this moment just for her.

I clear my throat, some sort of cosmic nudge from my sister telling me that sometimes you have to find the words, even when it's hard.

"Girls, I know I don't tell you often enough, but I'm proud of you and I love you."

Hallie runs over and hugs me. "And Suki, too."

Suki and I lock eyes as I say, "Suki, too."

"And Darling."

With a single note bark of laughter, I say, "I'm not sure about that."

"He's part of our family. You love your family."

"We got you and Darling a present!" The words spill out of Charlotte like she can't hold them in any longer.

"It was supposed to be a surprise, Charlotte!" Olivia snaps.

"It's okay, I'll still be surprised."

Charlotte searches beneath the tree and finds a box--holding it up. "Is this it, Suki?"

Suki squints, trying to see the tag. "If it says 'To Carter and Darling,' that's it.'"

"It does." Charlotte runs over to me with the box, her eyes bright with happiness.

It's wrapped in shiny silver paper adorned with shiny red and green ribbon. I open it and move aside the tissue paper, groaning.

There are two sweaters in the box, both red and cream, with snowflakes and reindeer.

"Matching sweaters!" Hallie cries like it's not obvious.

"Are you serious?" I mutter.

Suki is holding back a laugh. Olivia and Charlotte are already on the way to the stairs to find Darling.

"Put yours on, Uncle Carter!" Hallie begs.

I shake my head and give Suki an aggravated look. "No pictures."

"Yes pictures."

"If my teammates see those, they'll still be making fun of me when I'm eighty."

"You have to wear it, Uncle Carter." Hallie's tone is no-nonsense. "It's a present."

"You're getting a chicken suit for your birthday, Halls."

She giggles. "No, I'm not."

The girls are soon racing back downstairs, Darling waddling into the room in front of them. Suki helps them get Darling's sweater on, which fits him like a condom.

"It's a little snug," Suki says, kissing the top of his head. "But you're a growing boy, aren't you?"

I thought I'd get away with wearing the sweater over my T-shirt and pajama pants, but the girls insist I go change into jeans and a dress shirt so I'll have a collar beneath the sweater.

They've got Darling on the couch when I get back downstairs.

"He's not allowed on the couch," I remind them.

"Just for the picture," Olivia says.

"And then another one with you in a wingback chair," Suki says.

"This is ridiculous," I grumble.

I can't believe I agree to it, but I end up on the couch with Darling's front end on my lap. It takes a lot of coaxing from the girls and Suki to get me to smile.

"Girls, you get up there with them for a picture," Suki says.

"But you should be in it, too," Charlotte says.

Suki hesitates. I know what she's thinking. That this is the only Christmas she'll be part of our family.

"We'll do both," she says. "I'll take one and then use a timer for one of all of us."

I can't believe the girls would rather do these photos than tear into their gifts. Rachel and I would barely let our mom pee on Christmas mornings because we were so eager to open presents.

"Okay," Suki says when the photos are done. "Do you guys want to check out your stockings now?"

We have the stockings Rachel made for them. She was learning to quilt and she created a quilted stocking for each of them. Olivia's expression clouds with sadness as she looks at hers, running her fingers over the fabric.

"Those stockings are beautiful," Suki says gently.

"Our mom loved Christmas," Olivia says, her gaze on the stocking.

"Especially the Grinch," Charlotte says. "She made Grinch punch on Christmas and decorated our house with Grinch stuff."

I never went to Rachel's to spend Christmas with her and her girls. She invited me every year, and I'd send her gifts and a big check. I wish the pain I felt over that could be physical instead of emotional because it hurts in a way that's almost unbearable.

When I had the chance to be with them, I chose a workout and football instead. Maybe dinner with a teammate and his family. What a cold asshole I am. If I didn't have custody of the girls now, would I have ever spent a Christmas morning with them?

The silence stretches, Suki letting the girls sit with their feelings instead of glossing over them. Somehow she always knows when to soothe the pain and when to give it some space.

"It's Darling!" Hallie squeals with happiness and holds up a little stuffed pig.

Charlotte unwraps a gray beanie from her stocking next, grinning and putting it on.

The sadness slides away as the girls start opening all the little gifts Suki bought for their stockings, wrapped in tissue paper. I went shopping with her once, but she did a lot of it herself. She knows the girls' tastes better than I do.

I don't realize how much work she's done until I see the girls opening gift after gift, each item the perfect size and style. They all get a lot of clothes and they seem really happy about it.

"Uggs!" Olivia is giddy as she pulls a gray boot from a box. "I love them!"

I'm surprised when Suki hands me several gifts. She got me three new biographies, a travel reading light so I can read when I'm flying between cities, a nice leather messenger bag, two new ties and some 'Cereal Killer' socks.

She knows me. I've never had a relationship with a woman that didn't start with sex, so this is unfamiliar territory for me. All my other relationships were based around sex and sometimes we happened to get to know each other.

"This is amazing!" Suki holds up the T-shirt that Olivia picked out for her, which has a picture of Ruth Bader Ginsberg and says, "You Can't Handle the Ruth."

"You told us you love her, so I thought you'd like it." Olivia was very proud of finding that shirt online.

The girls helped me pick out all of Suki's gifts

other than the necklace. We got her a scarf, an avocado-shaped coffee mug and a spa gift certificate.

Once all the gifts are opened, Suki tells the girls to move their stuff to their rooms so Darling doesn't destroy anything. They're all upstairs and I'm picking up wrapping paper and stuffing it into a trash bag when she approaches me, running a fingertip over the vine on her necklace.

"This was so generous and sweet of you," she says softly. "I'm overwhelmed."

"I'm glad you like it."

Her expression turns to longing. I let go of the garbage bag and put a hand on her lower back, pulling her against me in a fluid motion.

Her eyes widen as she looks up at me, her lips slightly parted. I can't fight it anymore. I kiss her, only the first few seconds soft and slow. A little moan comes from her mouth as she melts into me, wrapping her arms around my neck.

She fits against me perfectly. Once I get a taste, my hunger for her is insatiable. I kiss her deeper, lifting her off her feet so we're molded together. She slides her fingers into my hair.

"Darling, no!"

Olivia's yell as she runs across the family room brings me back to reality and I set Suki down, her expression a little dazed.

When we look over at Darling, he has one of my new ties hanging from his mouth.

Of course. He's ruined three pairs of my shoes and destroyed the carpet in two rooms of the house. Might as well cockblock me, too.

CHAPTER FIFTEEN

Suki

I'M WAITING for my sandwich in a drive-through line when I get a text from Dex about the offer someone made me for the Naughty by Nature inventory.

Dex: It's low. I'd counter at $30k and then meet him in the middle at $25k.

My heart sinks. I text him back.

Suki: It cost $71k. You don't think I can get more?

Dex: You can try. I don't know anything about the market for secondhand sex toys.

Suki: They're new. Most of it is still in the manufacturer's packaging.

Dex: Still not considered new to a buyer, babe.

Suki: This really sucks. I think I'll sell them just so I

can stop fielding messages on Craigslist about it. People assume things about a woman selling thousands of vibrators, dildos, and butt plugs.

Dex: I mean...it's not an enviable position to be in.

Suki: Yeah, I just want to put this behind me.

Dex: Do you mean just the plugs, or the vibes and dildos, too...?

Suki: I hate you.

Dex: You practically mailed me an invitation to that one...Only accept a wire transfer as payment, ok?

I get my sandwich and drink and pull out of the drive-through and park before I text Dex again.

Suki: Yeah, and I'm making the buyer cover shipping. Can't wait to declare what I'm sending on the Customs forms. The buyer is in Denmark.

Dex: Do not ship the merch until you've been paid. I can write up a sales contract for you if you want.

Suki: That would be great. I hate you a little less.

Dex: Have to go babe, ttyl

I open my Italian melt and take a bite, checking my other texts. Mara sent one while I was driving.

Mara: I know I deflect with sarcasm, but this is me being real. I genuinely like Owen and I'm so nervous about this drink thing. If all I can get is sex, I'll take it, but if I give him sex right away, am I sending the message that it's all I want?

Suki: Ugh, of course not. Relationships start lots of

different ways. If he wants more, he'll want it whenever you guys have sex.

Mara: I know, but...I can't help wanting to do this right. If I go in there wearing a tiny little dress and I'm digesting his jizz by midnight, will he take me seriously?

Suki: Who are you and what have you done with Mara? We wear what we want. We suck what we want. And we don't slut shame.

Mara: Okay. You're right. Just because he's 46 doesn't mean he's old fashioned...right?

Suki: Right. It just means you might need to pump his dick up to get him hard.

Mara: This is serious, you wretched whore. And I can tell from his dick outline in his pants that he can get hard just fine.

Suki: Ew, what kind of pants is he wearing?

Mara: Irrelevant. I'm borrowing a dress from you.

Suki: Help yourself. Don't leave cum stains on this one, please and thanks.

Mara: I told you it wasn't a cum stain!

Suki: And I still don't believe you.

Mara: Have you heard from Carter?

Suki: Just usual stuff about schedules and the girls.

Mara: You should text him a tit pic...

Suki: I think the fuck not.

Mara: He kissed you and bought you a Tiffany necklace! He def wants to take you to Bonetown.

Suki: If he does it's because I'm the only woman he ever sees.

Mara: Bullshit! Pro athletes can get laid eight days a week if they want.

Suki: Maybe he's getting laid on the road.

Mara: You should ask him.

I set my phone down, eating the rest of my sandwich. I've been thinking about the kiss nonstop since it happened the day before yesterday. Kisses like that happen in movies, but I've never had one in real life.

He actually picked me up, his hand squeezing my ass and my core pressing against his erection. That kiss was hotter than the quickies I used to have with Tyler. And honestly, every sexual encounter we had was a quickie.

If we'd been alone in the house, I wouldn't have wanted to stop. That kiss made me feel like the most desirable woman in the world. But I'm already feeling a lot more for Carter than I expected, and sex would complicate things even more.

Tyler left me feeling broken and used. I made a promise to myself that I'd never feel that way again. And this arrangement with Carter is temporary. It's also not just me and him. The girls are part of it. I've noticed the way he looks at me sometimes when I'm with the girls.

He likes how much I love them, and vice versa.

But that's not enough to make jumping into bed together a good idea. Staying with me after the year is up would be ideal for Carter because I'd take care of the girls and he'd still be gone a lot of the time. He could fuck around with women and have the best of all worlds.

I'm not doing that.

I crumple up the wrapper from my sandwich and stuff it into the bag, then check my phone again.

Mara: So you don't want to ask him, just say that.

Suki: If I asked him, he'd say no and I wouldn't believe him. He takes quick showers at home and has no time to stroke his salami in there. I seriously doubt he just has months' worth of sperm backed up in his balls.

Mara: You can't just never trust a man again because of Fuckface.

Suki: I can, though. I have to go get groceries, talk later.

Mara: OK.

Carter's aunt Rosie flew in yesterday to spend a few days with us. She took the girls shopping for Christmas gifts today, and I'm using the time to run errands. We go through a lot of food with three growing girls and one growing pig.

I'm making beef stroganoff and homemade bread for dinner. Cooking a labor-intensive homemade meal and then cleaning the whole kitchen when I'm done is relaxing to me. I cook more when Carter is on the road, which is a change.

I used to prefer it when he was gone and it was just me and the girls. But now, I miss him when he's on the road. I lie in bed at night watching his games on my phone and wondering what he's doing afterward.

It's not a good idea for me to start an actual relationship with Carter, but the thought of him with other women makes me die a little inside.

This is definitely a curveball I don't know how to deal with. It snuck up on me, but I can't deny it anymore.

I have a crush on my husband.

CHAPTER SIXTEEN

Carter

BASH PASSES me the puck and I make a slap shot toward the net, someone crashing into me and knocking me to the ice before I can see whether it made it in.

The sound of the crowd tells me it did. I push myself out from underneath an opponent's leg and up from the ice.

I glance over and see that it was Cal Fournier who hit me. That guy's the least coordinated hockey player I've ever known; I have no idea how he managed to land on a pro roster.

My teammates surround me for a celebration. I tap gloves with them, wondering if Suki is watching a broadcast of the game. When I text her after games, she always knows whether we won or lost. If we win, she congratulates me. If we lose, she doesn't mention the game.

Once I'm back on the bench, I grab a towel and wipe down my sweaty face. Playing against Nashville is always intense. They almost score, Isaac diving in front of the goal and barely making a save.

"Saw your Christmas pictures," Bash says from beside me. "You and Darling look like a happy couple."

"Fuck off."

He laughs. "You gonna be mad at Leo over the pig for the rest of your life?"

"Probably."

"How big's it gonna get?"

"Two fifty to five hundred."

"Holy shit. What are you gonna do?"

I scowl, following the game. "What can I do? The girls love the damn thing."

"Does it smell?"

"No, pigs are actually clean. If they can't get to any mud."

Lucien snarls at one of the new Nashville players, throwing a glove to the ice and punching him in the face in about two seconds flat. The game stops while they trade punches, the opponent putting both arms up in an effort to protect himself.

"Who is that?" I ask Bash.

"Rookie. I don't remember his name. Weighs about a buck sixty."

Lucien doesn't unleash his worst on the kid; after about half a dozen punches, he skates over to the penalty box. The refs congregate to discuss the penalties.

I grab my water bottle and squeeze a shot of water into my mouth.

"What does Suki think about the pig?" Bash asks me.

"She says we can't get rid of it."

"You're stuck with it, then."

I sigh and shake my head. "I thought we'd be stuck with a twenty-five pound one. This fucker could crush me in my sleep. Or one of the girls."

"Maybe he needs his own room."

I shoot him a glare. "Don't suggest that around Suki or the girls. I'm not paying for a pig room."

He scoffs. "You really trusted Leo to handle this?"

Leo leans forward from nearby us on the bench, and looks at me. "I said I was sorry about the confusion. You wanted a little pig and I found you a little pig."

"A *micro* pig, you dipshit. I have a farm hog living in my house now."

The sound of the whistle makes me turn and focus on the game again. I can't let myself get distracted until it's over. If I don't give a game a hundred percent of my attention, little things slide and I make mistakes.

I've just stopped actively sweating when we change lines and I go back in. I can feel the couple of workouts I missed on Christmas Eve and Christmas as I dig to get up and down the ice. After the debacle that was Thanksgiving, Suki told her family we wanted a low-key Christmas at home this year with just the five of us.

It was perfect. She made a roast and we all stayed in our pajamas all day. Or rather, I stayed in the pajama pants I changed back into and my sweater because the girls insisted I wear it for the entire day.

I haven't had a Christmas like that since I was a kid. I thought about my mom and Rachel, and I think Suki thought of her family, too. It was the first time she'd ever not seen her family on Christmas, and she did that for me and the girls.

I've never been with a woman who didn't put her wants first. Even when Kaia flew to Cleveland for my games, it was about her. She wanted to be seen and photographed before and after the games, preferably with me. Everything she did was in pursuit of her ultimate goal--a pro athlete husband.

Suki does a hundred little things a day for me and the girls just because it's who she is. When she makes spaghetti, Olivia gets plain sauce instead of meat sauce. Every time I have a home game, I come home to a plate of grilled chicken and vegetables in the fridge, my favorite postgame meal.

I know I'm in deep with her because it feels even better to do things for her. I felt like a rock star when she opened the necklace. And when I kissed her, it was raw, real desire pouring from her. None of that fake bullshit I'm used to from women.

That kiss has been on my mind since the second it ended. Even now, I have to force my mind not to wander to the way she felt in my arms. I haven't had sex in more than six months and every bit of my pent-up sexual energy is focused on Suki.

My wife. It no longer sounds crazy like it did at first.

We edge out a 3–2 win and I'm still full of energy as we head to the visiting locker room. As soon as I get to my phone, I find a text from Suki.

Suki: Great game! Darling snorted his approval when you scored.

She attached a picture of her and Darling in bed, her in a white tank top with her hair fanned out on the pillow and him snuggled up to her chest.

I'm jealous of him. His snout is just casually resting on her breast. I'd give my left nut to be there right now.

I text her back.

Carter: Thanks. It'll be good to get home.

What I mean is it'll be good to get home to her, but we're still doing a dance where we don't say things like that. I'm tired of the dance. What I really want to say is *ditch the pig, put on something sexy and wait for me to come bury my face in your pussy.*

Damn, would it be nice to get into bed to find her ready to finish what we started with the kiss. I ache for it. I've seen so many of her facial expressions, from surprised to amused to exhausted. I've heard her laugh, be gentle but stern with the girls and be firm with Darling. But what does she look like when she's about to come? What does she sound like when she does?

I've never seen so many sides of a woman I wanted while still panting after her like a fucking dog. I want that last part of Suki I'm missing, and I want it bad.

"Your tub's ready," one of our trainers tells me.

I nod, strip down and head for the ice bath. When I step in, my thoughts of Suki are frozen away.

Ice baths are great for recovery but not so great for fantasizing about what it would feel like for your wife to ride you until she milks you dry.

Our flight home takes an hour and a half, and I'm climbing the stairs to get to the bedroom around 1:45 a.m. The closer I get to Suki, the harder my dick gets.

I can't do it like this, waking her up in the middle of the night, but I also can't continue wanting her so badly and not acting on it.

When I switch on the bathroom light, it casts a faint glow into the bedroom and I see Darling in the middle of the bed, his back to Suki's chest.

That lucky bastard. If I felt her tits against my back right now, I'd probably shoot my load. Six months plus with no sex is basically a medical condition.

I strip down to boxer briefs and get in bed, pushing one of Darling's hooves out of my way.

Now to see if I can actually sleep. Tomorrow's the day we've been waiting for--the hearing when the judge will decide if Chad gets the girls or I do.

Through my attorney, I offered him two weeks with them every summer because she advised me that the judge would want them to have at least some contact with him if he wanted it.

I'm a wreck over it, which is another reason I'm

not waking Suki up to tell her I've got perpetual blue balls over her. This isn't the time.

Tomorrow, I'll either find out I get to keep the girls, or I'll be devastated. That has to be my priority.

But whichever way it goes, I want Suki to stay in my life. It's a sobering thought that it might not be "our lives" anymore. The thought of me and Suki here without the girls is something I can't even wrap my head around.

The minutes tick by and I stare up at the dark ceiling, absently petting the top of Darling's head as I try not to imagine telling the girls they have to move to Alaska to live with the father they don't even know.

CHAPTER SEVENTEEN

Suki

THE HEARING WAS SET for ten, but we're still sitting in the hallway outside the courtroom waiting at 10:35 a.m.

Carter shifts in his seat beside me, checking his watch again. Even though he got home in the middle of the night, he was already in the kitchen when I got up at six thirty this morning, coffee brewed and breakfast cooking.

The girls didn't know about this hearing, so they were their usual morning selves. Olivia was ready to go early, Charlotte was running late and Hallie had to give Darling a dozen kisses and hugs before walking out the door.

178

Carter did school drop-off, then he came home and dressed in a dark suit with one of the ties I got him for Christmas. I'm wearing black pants and a simple green blouse, my hair in a knot at the nape of my neck.

I pat his knee reassuringly and he takes my hand in his, lacing our fingers together. Neither one of us could eat and we both drank too much coffee; it's hard just sitting here and feeling helpless.

Carter nodded toward the girls' father, Chad, when he sat down in a seat on the other side of the hallway. He's average-looking, dressed in khakis and a dress shirt. Charlotte looks like him.

It's all I can do to ignore him. I want to go ask him how he could ignore his own children. I'd miss the girls if they were gone for a weekend. I can't even fathom not seeing them for years. He's a failure as a parent and as a human.

Finally, a bailiff opens the courtroom doors and Carter's attorney, Michelle, stands up, gesturing for us to follow.

I sit in one of the rows of benches for spectators. Carter and Michelle sit at one of the tables facing the judge's bench and Chad sits at the other table, a man who must be his attorney beside him.

I'm trying to calm my racing heart with deep breathing when the door to the judge's chambers opens and she walks out. Everyone stands while she walks to her seat and then she tells us to be seated.

Carter sits stiff-backed as the judge talks about reports from counselors and teachers and filings from the attorneys. She asks Carter some questions and then asks Chad some questions.

I'm shocked to learn that Chad's wife already has three kids and is pregnant with another one. If the girls are sent to live with him, there will be seven kids in a three-bedroom home.

"We could use some of Rachel's life insurance money to buy a bigger house," he tells the judge.

Carter doesn't move. His attorney told him not to show any reaction to anything, no matter how outrageous. I know it's taking all his self-control to stay silent.

"I can't order money locked up in trusts to be distributed to you," the judge tells Chad. "If your attorney advised you that was an option, you were misinformed."

Chad clears his throat. "I thought that money was for the girls to be taken care of."

"Mr. Stanton put all the money into trusts for the children."

Chad looks over at Carter. "Well, I'm not a millionaire like him."

"Money aside," the judge says, "I've decided the

children should remain with Mr. Stanton and his wife. If Mr. Bailey wishes to come to Cleveland to visit the children, he may do so, with those details to be worked out between the parties. Mr. Bailey will also get two uninterrupted weeks of visitation every summer at his home if he wishes. I also want him to be allowed regular phone contact with the children. To have access to pictures of them and to receive communications about their grades and activities. Are you willing to do those things, Mr. Stanton?"

"Yes. Thank you, your honor."

"All the teachers and counselors have said the girls are doing well with you. Keep doing what you're doing. And Mr. Bailey, had you been active in the children's lives before their mother's death, my decision may have been different."

The hearing ends then, with Carter hugging Michelle and Chad looking disgusted. I breathe a huge sigh of relief, smiling when Carter comes toward me, opening his arms.

"Thank God," he says softly. "We did it."

We hold onto each other for a solid minute, and then he pulls away and leans his forehead against mine. The excitement I felt when he kissed me on Christmas returns.

"Let's go home," I say softly.

———

"I WANT to take you on a date," Carter says when we're almost home. "Maybe Mara or Dex would be able to babysit. I can find someone else if not."

"Mara, Dex and Harry will fight over who gets to do it. If they're not busy, all three of them will come."

"If you want to, so will you."

I wrinkle my brow, confused. "So will I what?"

"Come."

My lips part and my face warms.

"I want you so fucking bad, Suki. It's all I can think about."

My whole body heats in response to his words. A relationship isn't in the cards for me, but sex? I'm not meant for the abstinent life.

"Do you mean after we go on a date--or now?" I ask.

"Both."

I laugh at his eagerness. "We do have cause for celebration."

The Navigator speeds up as he presses on the gas pedal. He looks over at me, hunger swirling in his dark-brown eyes.

"It's been a while for me, so I'll have to pace myself."

My heart soars as he confirms he hasn't been sleeping with women while traveling. "How long?"

"More than six months."

"Yeah, same."

I'm wearing my blouse with the top two buttons undone. I reach for the third one and unfasten it. Then, the fourth.

"Oh fuck." Carter looks over at me. "Don't make me wreck the car."

"I thought you might like a preview."

"I've had two months of previews every time you walk out of the shower in one of those tank tops. Or wear my jersey. You wore a black V-neck shirt once that I jerked off thinking about for days."

"A shirt?" I smile. "You're easy, Mr. Stanton."

"It was more about your tits in the shirt. Your tits are unbelievable."

He turns onto his street, the tires squealing. I can't keep myself from smiling; I had no idea I had this effect on him.

Before he turns into the driveway, he's pressing the button for the garage door opener. He slides to a stop in the garage, practically flying out of the car.

I open my door and step out, and he meets me in front of the passenger door. He takes my face in his hands and kisses me, backing me against the car door. His tongue brushes over mine, his erection pressing into my belly as we kiss each other like it's the last kiss we'll ever get.

We're both breathless when we pull apart, and Carter sweeps me up with an arm behind my knees. He carries me into the house, Darling trotting toward us happily.

"I don't care what he destroyed or ate. We're ignoring it," Carter murmurs.

He races up the stairs, not even winded, when he kicks the bedroom door closed and sets me on the bed.

I push myself right back out of it, finishing the last of the buttons on my blouse and dropping it to the floor with my shoes and pants. He's stripping off his clothes at the same time; he's down to boxer briefs when he walks over to the closet and comes back out with a box of condoms in hand.

He tosses it on the bed and takes me in his arms again. I gasp from the feel of his warm, taut body against mine. He groans as he unfastens my bra and takes it off, cupping one of my breasts and kissing my neck.

I've never been with a man his size. He's tall, broad and rock hard. I slide my hand to the front of his boxer briefs and stroke my hand down the front to size him up.

Wow. He's huge there, too. His ragged groan

empowers me to run my hand up and down his length again.

"Fuck," he mutters.

He puts a leg between mine, forcing me onto the bed. I lie back and he pulls my underwear off in a fluid motion, then bends so he's over my thighs, slowly working his way up them with kisses.

Gasps, moans and half giggles spill from my mouth as he tickles and teases me. When he runs the tip of his tongue down my seam, I cry out. It seems to urge him on, and soon he's licking and sucking like a starving man.

He holds nothing back, using his mouth and fingers to work my body right to the edge. But instead of letting me tip over, he stops, takes off his boxer briefs and rolls a condom over his erection.

He fills me up before he's all the way in, stretching me. But it's still good, and I spread my legs wider. Once he's all the way in, he closes his eyes, then opens them and kisses me softly.

"Tell me if I do anything you don't like," he says.

"Just don't stop."

He pulls out and pushes himself all the way back in, both of us groaning with pleasure. I wrap my legs around him and he picks up the pace, building me up with every thrust.

It's beyond good. It's bliss having this massive

man focused entirely on fucking me. Just the sight and sound of his pleasure is bringing me close to coming.

"Yes, like that," I say, my voice breathy. "Don't stop."

He does exactly what I want. The only sounds in the room are our bodies slamming together and our heavy breathing.

"Oh, God." I grip his back tighter as I reach the edge, crying out his name as I come. "Carter! Please don't stop."

I come hard, the orgasm extended by his powerful groan as he thrusts into me a final time and comes, too. We're both breathless when he rolls off me, picking up my hand and kissing the back of it.

"That's the way everything should be celebrated," I say, my voice relaxed and happy.

"Hell yes. You make me crazy in the best way."

"We just consummated our marriage," I say, realizing it as the words come out.

"I'm not sure it took. We should probably do it again."

I laugh, propping myself up on an elbow so I can see his face. "If it's that good every time, we can do it as many times as you want."

CHAPTER EIGHTEEN

Carter

"OH...CARTER."

I can tell from her tone that Suki finds waking up to my mouth on her pussy better than her alarm.

It's been less than twenty-four hours since we had sex for the first time. After taking the girls out for dinner last night and watching *Megamind* in the basement home theater, I locked the bedroom door once the girls were in bed. Suki and I spent hours discovering each other in bed.

We've had sex seven times already, but I still can't get enough of her. I slept a few hours last night and woke up this morning rock hard and thinking about her.

The glide of my tongue into her pussy makes her moan and rake her fingertips over my scalp, gripping my hair. I push her thighs open wider and back, opening her up.

She's so damn responsive, her pussy wet and her clit swollen. I tease it with the tip of my tongue and she gasps. Then I suck on it, causing her to roll her hips and press down on my head.

"Mm." I plant a kiss on her clit. "Feels good when you fuck my face."

I slide two fingers inside her and flatten my tongue over her clit, wishing I had more time. But it was 6:18 a.m. when I woke up and checked the time on my phone. And her alarm will go off at six thirty. So I lick and suck and finger fuck her until she comes against my mouth, her hips arched up off the bed as she tries to hold in her cries of pleasure.

When she drops back to the mattress with a deep, satisfied sigh, I wipe my hand over my mouth and lie next to her, propped on one elbow.

"Morning," I say, grinning.

She laughs softly. "That was amazing. Now let's get to your turn because the sun's coming up and I have to get up soon."

I kiss her cheek. "That *was* my turn. I got what I wanted."

"What time is it?"

I pick up my phone. "Six twenty-eight. Couldn't have timed that better."

She picks up her phone and turns off the alarm. "We have time."

"It's okay. You have to get the girls up and I'm jumping in the shower."

She slept in one of my Crush T-shirts, and she gets out of bed and pulls it up and off over her head. "I'm taking a shower myself. You can take one with me if you're willing to bend me over and fuck me, or you can wait for your turn."

Fuck. I'm all the way hard now. My gaze rakes up and down her body. I wanted to show her I'm not selfish in bed and that pleasing her pleases me, too. But it's impossible to say no when she's looking at me like that, her hair messy and her nipples pebbled.

"I want you to use me and come hard." She looks at me over her shoulder. "Only think about getting yourself off."

"You like that?"

She nods. "Tell me I'm a whore and fuck me like you mean it. I'll be fantasizing about it all day."

Holy hell. Hearing those words from sweet, nurturing Suki makes my cock ache. I'm out of bed and on my way to the bathroom in less than a second.

When I walk into the room, she's just turned on

the water and she's giving me a seductive smile, gently pinching both nipples.

I slide off my underwear and step out of them, locking the bathroom door.

"You sure about this?" I ask, palming my cock.

"I'm sure I want it. Not so sure you'll give it to me."

Jesus, she's going to kill me. She turns to step into the shower and I take her hips, moving her toward me.

"Not there." I turn her to face the double vanity.

She takes a couple steps toward it and I put a palm on her back, pushing it down. "You told me last night you're on birth control, so you're getting it all today. Starting your day off with a pussy full of cum."

She gasps and spreads her feet apart slightly. I run my fingers through her soaking pussy and then rub my cock, pushing it inside her with one hard thrust. She moans, her palms flat on the counter.

"Such a tight, sweet pussy. Made for my cock." I hold on to her hips, pounding into her. "No shower for you after this. My whore keeps my cum in her little cunt. I want you to feel it running out of you and remember who you belong to."

"Oh my God."

She pushes herself up slightly, her gaze finding

mine in the mirror. I slam into her again, already on the edge of coming. I grab a handful of her hair and pull her head back, making her rise slightly so I can see her tits shaking while I fuck her.

I've never seen a sexier woman in my life. She's perfect.

"That ring on your finger means you're my whore."

Her eyes widen and she moves a hand down between her legs. I put a thumb in my mouth, soaking it before running it around her back hole. She moans hard as I slide it in her, fucking her as hard as my hips can.

"What does the ring mean?" I ask her in a strained voice, holding back my orgasm.

"That...I'm your whore. Oh fuck. Carter, I'm coming."

Her lips part and our eyes meet, my balls slapping against her one last time as I come so hard I'm lightheaded for a second. My whole body goes slack and I lean against her, kissing her shoulder as I catch my breath.

"Wow." She moves from in front of the sink.

"Hey." I tip her chin up until our gazes meet. "Are you good?"

She smiles. "Am I good? That was the best orgasm I've ever had."

I feel like a fucking god right now. "Have you ever asked for dirty talk before?"

"No. I've never been with anyone who would have done it."

I might as well just drop to my knees and worship her. She's my fucking fantasy come to life.

"I'll get as dirty as you want, but you have to promise you'll tell me if it's too much."

"It won't be. This is my hottest fantasy."

I shake my head and kiss her softly. "How did I manage to sleep next to you for two months without doing this?"

She arches a brow. "Just don't let that happen again."

I smile. "I don't have a chance of keeping my hands off you now."

Raising her left hand to my lips, I kiss the oval solitaire diamond ring I put on her finger when we were married. Dex picked it out, and now I'm wishing I would have done that myself.

"Have a nice shower." She grins and kisses my cheek, walking out of the bathroom.

I look in the mirror, turning my face to the side and then to the other side. Who is this guy staring back at me? He's an uncle who might as well be a dad, and he's married to a woman who checks every box he's ever had and then some. This guy has a family, and he's pretty damn happy about it.

I didn't plan on having any of this until I was closer to forty. But I wouldn't change it if I could. I'm damn lucky that the woman I asked to marry me when I hardly knew her turned out to be incredible in every way.

It's time to drop all the pretenses and shred the contract. This relationship is the real thing, and I know Suki feels it, too.

CHAPTER NINETEEN

Suki

EVEN PUTTING away the laundry is better when you're having lots of great sex. I can't help smiling as I stack clean, folded pairs of pants in Hallie's dresser.

I hired an artist to paint a mural on one wall of her bedroom, but we're still deciding what kind of mural she wants. Her first choice was a mural of Darling with a unicorn horn and a tutu.

Carter was...less than keen on the idea. I told Hallie a mural isn't something we'll be changing anytime soon, and it needs to be something she will want in her room for the next few years. She insists she could never tire of anything with Darling on it. We're at an impasse.

I pick up the toys scattered on her floor and put them in the basket in the corner.

When I get to Charlotte's room, she's lying in bed with headphones on, watching something on her iPad. I stack her clean laundry on her dresser for her to put away herself.

Olivia has started doing her own laundry, so I don't even have to stop by her room. She's over at a friend's house for the afternoon.

It's Sunday, which is becoming my favorite day of the week. I have a beef roast in the slow cooker to make beef enchiladas out of for dinner. Now that the laundry is done, I have about an hour to read.

Picking up little bits of hay from the floor doesn't even bug me today because I am a thoroughly sexed woman. Orgasms are a daily thing instead of a rarity, like a full moon. I get it all: dirty talk, kisses, poundings and snuggles.

And I've learned my lesson on the hay. I got rid of it because it's too messy. I wanted Darling to have some of the things outdoor pigs have, but he'll have to settle for just his romps in the mud.

He's currently caked in it after rolling around in mud during an unusually warm January day on our walk earlier. I normally give him baths, but since today is Carter's day off, I delegated it to him.

There was only a split second of hesitation before

he agreed. He knows better than to bite the hand that jerks him.

When I walk into the family room, humming "Shake It Off" by Taylor Swift, I stop the moment I see Carter and Hallie.

He's sitting on the floor with his legs crossed in front of him, his back against the couch and his gaze on the big-screen TV. Hallie is sitting on a little stool beside him, using dark pink lipstick to color Carter's nose.

It looks like she went through an entire tube. She drew hearts on his cheeks with it and colored in his entire forehead. His eyelids are covered in something blue and glittery. She used the lipstick to draw long earrings down his earlobes to the side of his neck.

"Doesn't Uncle Carter look beautiful?" Hallie says, grinning.

"Um...yes, he does."

Carter glances at me. "She wanted to give me a makeover and I said she could if I could watch the game while she does it."

I arch my brows and reach into the pocket of my lightweight sweatpants for my phone.

"Can I get a picture of you two?"

Carter lowers his brows. "Only if it stays on your phone and is never posted anywhere."

"Okay, deal."

Hallie looks proud of her makeup artistry as she sits down in Carter's lap, putting an arm around his shoulder. He smiles, too. I feel a pang of wishing Rachel could see this.

"Okay, got my new screensaver," I say lightly.

I walk into the kitchen, Darling following me. He's wearing a doggie onesie covered with tacos today. I have to get in all the cute outfits I can before he outgrows the largest size made for dogs.

"Are you hungry, D-man? Do you want a snackie?"

He knows that word well. He snorts in approval and goes over to the pantry.

"Not this time," I say, opening the refrigerator and taking out a container.

I've started keeping pureed pumpkin, roasted sweet potatoes and squash prepped for him. He doesn't like them as much as Goldfish, but he doesn't turn them down.

I fix him a plate and set it on the floor. He walks over to it, sniffs it, and then looks back at me.

"That's my only offer," I say, shrugging.

He scarfs it. I leave him in the kitchen and go up to the bedroom, eagerly anticipating my hour of reading.

Before I started working two jobs, I read every

night. With two jobs, I was too tired. After a full day of caring for the girls and Darling, I'm usually too mentally tired to read. I either watch Carter's games or scroll mindlessly until I fall asleep.

I lie down and open up the sci-fi romance paperback I've heard great things about. I'm about fifteen minutes into it when Carter comes into the bedroom, closing the door behind him.

"How's it going?" he asks.

"Good. How are you?"

He gestures at his face. "I'm gonna go wash this off."

"Aw, what about Hallie's hard work?"

"I let her take a picture. I never agreed to leave this shit on my face for hours."

He goes into the bathroom and I hear him turn on the shower. Less than ten minutes later, he comes back into the bedroom, his face clean and his hair damp. He's wearing a gray Penn State T-shirt and black athletic shorts. I like him this way, wearing his casual, around-the-house clothes that the rest of the world doesn't get to see.

He lies down on his side, looking at me. "You're sexy when you read."

I look away from my book, smiling at him. "I feel like I'm sexy when you're horny."

"I'm horny a hundred percent of the time, so that tracks."

"Are you angling for a quickie?"

"Nah. Not with the girls awake."

"Maybe later."

He hums his disapproval. "Won't be a quickie, though. Take a nap and a multivitamin, baby, 'cause I need to make up for all the nights I'll miss with you on my next road trip."

Tyler used to call me "baby." It feels different from Carter, but I still feel the stab of betrayal and anger I get every time I think of Tyler.

"I'm going back to the game," he says, getting out of bed.

"Hey, don't forget Darling's bath."

He groans. "Fuck. Fine. If you aren't sure how much I love you, that should say it all."

My heart pounds faster and I meet his gaze. He looks a little alarmed, but then his expression softens.

"Yeah. I do love you, Suki. I wanted to talk to you about us, actually." He stands at the foot of the bed, crossing his arms. "This isn't a one-year thing anymore. I want you to stay."

My brows shoot up. "Stay?"

Aggravation flickers over his face for a split second before he schools his expression back to neutral. "Yeah. Neither one of us is faking anything anymore. I love our family and I want it to be permanent. Don't you feel the same way?"

I set my book down and take a deep breath. "Where is this coming from? It's only been a couple of months and we just started sleeping together a few days ago."

He knits his brows together, the aggravated expression back. "So what? I don't need any more time to know what I want."

I pull my knees up to my chest, emotions warring inside me. I swore to myself I'd never blindly fall hard and fast for a man again. I was so depressed and humiliated after Tyler left me it took months to start feeling like myself again.

"I love the girls, and I probably love you, too. But I—"

"Probably?" He pinches the bridge of his nose. "What the fuck, Suki? I've done everything the right way. I haven't even looked at another woman, I spend all my free time with you guys and I got you something nice for Christmas. What more do you want from me?"

I just look at him in disbelief. "Do you seriously think you get to decide this for me? Because you *haven't looked at another woman for two months*, you spend all your free time at home—which you should do, Carter, it doesn't make you a saint—and you bought me some jewelry?"

"It's more than I've done for any other woman." His tone is laced with bitterness, fueling my anger.

"I don't care about other women. We got married because you *needed* me. It had nothing to do with your feelings for me."

He puts his hands on his hips, scowling. "I didn't have any feelings for you then. I do now."

"Good for fucking you. What about *my* feelings?"

He scoffs. "Guess it's good I'm seeing this side of you now. What the fuck? I tell you I love you and this is your reaction? Fuck me, it's all about you?"

My pulse pounds as I walk closer to him, lowering my voice so the girls can't hear our argument.

"True or false, Carter? Your feelings for me are at least partially based on how much the girls love me."

He narrows his eyes. "What's that supposed to mean?"

"Answer the question."

"Yeah, it's true. I love how you are with them. You're the best thing that's happened to them since they lost their mom."

Tears spring to my eyes. It feels amazing to know he thinks that, but it also clouds his feelings for me.

"I don't want you to be with me just because I'm a

great choice to help you raise the girls." I fight back the tears pooling in my eyes. "I want someone who is completely madly in love with me. Who wants me and no one else."

"I want you and no one else."

"How can you know that after two months in a fake marriage?"

He shrugs. "I just do."

"What if you don't feel that way in six months? Or in two years?"

"How can anyone know how they'll feel in two years?"

I swipe the tears from the corners of my eyes. "Everything was going so well. Why did you have to blow it up like that?"

His eyes bulge. "Blow it up? By telling you I'm not faking it anymore and I really do want you to keep being my wife? By telling you I love you? And then you tell me you *probably* love me. But I'm the one who blew it up."

"I'm not getting burned again." My voice breaks with emotion. "You want me to jump in with both feet a few *days* after we started this thing for real. That's not fair."

"I'm not him, Suki. Judge me for my actions alone."

"I'm not the starry-eyed twenty-two-year-old I

was when I met him. We're shaped by the things that happen to us, good and bad."

With a bitter one-note hum, he says, "So I have to deal with you not trusting me because of what he did. I have to fix what he broke. Is that what you're saying?"

His being pissed off about my brokenness is the final straw for me. I point at the closet.

"One of us is packing a bag and going somewhere else for the night. Is it me or you?"

"Oh, okay. Now you want me to leave my own house?"

I walk over to the closet. "No problem, I'll go."

He follows me inside. "I'll fucking go. I have to be at the arena in the morning anyway. I'll stay at Bash's."

I walk out of the closet and out of the bedroom, needing to get away from him. I can't believe how cold and harsh he was. All because I didn't fall at his feet like he expected me to.

Fuck him. If he can't meet me where I'm at and respect how I got here, I'm not even faking a relationship with him anymore. I won't be able to stand even looking at him.

CHAPTER TWENTY

Carter

"HEY MAN, do you have a charger I can borrow?"

Bash doesn't look up from his phone as he asks the question. Our flight home from a shitty road trip is landing in twenty minutes, and his question sets me off.

"Get your ass on Amazon and place an order for ten fucking chargers, Bash. Or thirty. Put at least a dozen of them in your travel bag so you're not asking me for one every fucking time we step onto a plane or a bus."

"Dude, just tell Suki you're sorry and make up with her. You're crankier than a woman on her period and I'm fucking done."

I scoff. "Ha! You're done? You're the one who's twenty-seven years old and can't even keep track of a phone charger. Or drop off your dry cleaning. Or take a break from video games to go visit your goddamn grandma."

"It was the first day the game came out and I went the next day, asshole."

I press my lips together and ignore him. The tension between us started when I went to stay with him on the day Suki kicked me out of my own house and I told him the truth about our marriage.

He sided with her, and we might have gotten into a minor wrestling match over it. Then I had to sleep in his guest room on a bed with no sheets because the dipshit just covered it with a comforter and called it a day.

Our road trip was a back-to-back. Where we play a game in one city one night and another city the next. They're always a grind. I wanted to call or text Suki, but my pride wouldn't let me, so we haven't spoken since Sunday.

We lost both games on the road trip and our goalie, Isaac, injured his wrist in the first one. Charlotte's been texting me that Olivia is crying all the time over some boy, which makes me want to crush that boy with my bare hands.

I just want to get home. Charlotte told me Suki

left a couple of hours ago and Harry's at the house with them, which has to mean she's still avoiding me.

Every hour of every day since she said it, I've replayed her saying she "probably" loves me. There I was, pouring my guts out about wanting to be with her, and she stabbed me in the gut.

Fuck probably. In fact, fuck everything. As soon as the bus, which is taking us from the airport back to the player parking lot at the arena, stops, I stand up. I get off as quickly as I can, not saying a word to anyone.

There's enough snow on the ground that it crunches beneath my shoes as I walk to my car. I hope Suki's ancient Toyota Camry still starts in this ice-cold weather. I'm pissed at her, but I still don't want her stranded on the side of the road. She was driving my Navigator most of the time because the girls liked it better, and I was driving my Jeep Wrangler to the arena for road trips. But Charlotte told me Suki drove her own car when she left this afternoon.

Just one more *fuck you*, I guess. Women are goddamn impossible. I tried to just say *fuck it, who needs her anyway*, but that only lasted about forty-five seconds.

I need her. And the girls do, too.

I brush the snow off the Wrangler's windshield while it warms up. It's still cold when I get inside. The fatigue of a back-to-back hits me as I drive home. We stayed in Vancouver last night after our game, but I slept like shit. When I finally did fall asleep, I dreamed that Suki had told me she married Tyler.

Harry's navy BMW is parked in the driveway when I pull into my garage. I need some peace and a nap.

I get my bag from the passenger seat and walk into the house, immediately hearing someone wailing.

Hallie. I put my bag down and rush into the family room. Hallie's sobbing, her hands over her face, and Charlotte looks stunned. Olivia is standing next to Harry, looking anguished, his arm around her shoulders in reassurance.

"Olivia lost Darling," Charlotte says when she sees me.

"Lost him?"

Olivia's voice breaks with emotion when she starts to speak. "I took him for a walk. He saw a dog and pulled on the leash. I couldn't hold on to it."

"He's going to die!" Hallie wails.

"When did this happen?"

Harry's brows are knitted with concern.

"Olivia just got home like three minutes ago. We were about to get in my car and go look for him."

"I'll go. Liv, you come with me since you know where you were walking him."

"Can I come?" Charlotte asks.

"No, you stay here."

"He's going to freeze," Hallie says, sniffling.

"He has a coat and boots on," Olivia says.

"What about his snout?"

I put up a palm. "Let us get out of here and find him, okay? He's not exactly fast. He can only book it briefly and then he wears out."

"I called Suki. She's on her way," Charlotte says.

I nod, not wanting to leave now that I know that. But I have to. The girls love Darling, especially Hallie. I've got to find that fat fucker.

Olivia and I get in the Navigator, her expression solemn.

"Do you really think we'll find him?" she asks.

"Yep. I'm not lucky enough to get rid of him this easily."

"Uncle Carter!"

I shake my head and sigh. "He's grown on me a little bit, I guess. Everyone in the neighborhood has seen us walking him and they know he's ours because no one else is insane enough to have a farm animal in their house. If someone finds him, they'll bring him back."

"What if he just lies down and gives up on life? He could freeze to death."

I scrunch my face in confusion. "He's a pig, Liv. Why would he want to give up being petted and fed Goldfish and cupcakes?"

"I chased him for a while, but I was afraid I'd get lost. He went into the woods at the end of that cul-de-sac with the house that has a guest cottage."

"Okay." I drive in the direction of the cul-de-sac. "What's this I hear about you crying over a boy?"

"Ugh, did Charlotte tell you?"

"Don't worry about who told me."

"Only Suki and Charlotte know, and Suki wouldn't betray me."

"Okay, drama queen. What happened?"

She shrugs. "He doesn't like me. That's it. And now he knows I like him and it's embarrassing."

"He needs to get some glasses. Any guy should consider himself lucky you like him."

A smile tugs at her lips. "Thanks. I thought you'd be mad that I like a boy."

"No, of course not. You can like boys as long as you stay at least six feet away from them at all times."

"Are you serious?"

"Absolutely."

"It's him!" Her face lights up and she points out the passenger window. "He's okay."

Darling is walking in someone's front yard, his snout to the ground as he explores. I'm more relieved than I thought I would be.

I park in front of the house and we both get out of the car. Darling lifts his head and looks at us.

"Darling, come on!" Olivia says. "Let's go home."

He turns and walks in the opposite direction of us, his leash dragging through the snow.

"Darling!" I call. "Come on, dude, it's cold out here."

We jog toward him. As soon as he sees me, he speeds up. I stop and shake my head.

"We can't let him get away!" Olivia says as she runs to catch up with him.

It's freezing out here and I'm missing my nap. I run faster this time, catching up to him. I bend down to pick his leash up, but he darts away.

"You bastard," I mutter.

Olivia tries to grab him, but he eludes her, too.

"Let's try to box him in," I call out.

I get on one side of him and try to close in, making Darling run toward her. He does, but when he gets close to her, he dodges to the side.

He's just jogging until we get close. He's surprisingly fast when he wants to be.

"Treaties!" Olivia yells. "Want treaties, Darling?"

He stops and looks at her. I creep toward him, stepping as quietly as I can.

"Let's go home and get treaties," Olivia says, crouching down. "Want some Goldfish?"

He heads toward her, snuffling with excitement. I get close enough to grab his leash and I pick it up.

"Good boy, Darling," Olivia says, hugging him.

"He's not a good boy. He only wants treats."

"Well, at least we caught him."

I walk him over to my car, and when we get there, a guy is standing in his yard, filming us with his camera phone. Fucking great. I really don't want the world to know I have a pet pig who wears a puffer coat and dog boots.

I ignore the guy filming and tell Olivia to get in the car. She does, and I pick Darling up to put him in the back seat. He squeals loudly, making it look and sound like I'm stabbing him or something. This isn't unusual; he hates being carried.

"I swear I'll put you on a sandwich," I grumble under my breath. "Get your ass in the car."

I manage to get him onto the seat, put the leash in the car and close the door.

"Can I see him?" I hear Hallie saying when I get in the car.

"I FaceTimed her," Olivia says to me.

She points her phone toward the back seat. "There he is."

"My darling!" Hallie cries.

"Hi, Darling."

That voice belongs to Suki. I turn the car around quickly and step on the gas, eager to get home and see her.

"Did you have an adventure?" Olivia asks Darling. "Are you hungry?"

I let go of my irritation over freezing my balls off chasing the pig. It was his getting away from Olivia that made Suki come back. I want her to stay.

When I come home from a road trip, it's to Suki and the girls. I was a dick when I made coming home to them sound like some sort of accomplishment, but I'm not a charming man. I'm a direct communicator, not a game player.

Hopefully she cooled off during our time apart. I definitely did. I'm disappointed she's not all in like I am, but if she needs more time, I'll have to be okay with that.

When we get back to the house, Suki's car isn't there.

"Where's Suki?" I say out loud.

Olivia types out a text and then waits a couple of seconds. "Charlotte says she just left."

"For fuck's sake," I mumble.

"Are you guys having a fight?"

I don't want her to worry about it, so I say, "We're fine. Just working through something."

I pull into the garage, Hallie standing there waiting for us. As soon as I park the car, she opens the rear driver's side door and greets Darling with hugs and kisses.

At least she's happy. I'm sure as hell not.

CHAPTER TWENTY-ONE

Suki

"I MEAN, sloths do everything slow, right? They probably take, like, several days to digest their food," Dex says.

He looks around the table, studying my face, then Harry's, and then Mara's.

"I have no idea," Harry says, putting his hands up.

"Just guess three days," Mara says.

"Three days?" Dex looks at me. "Are you good with that?"

I shrug. "Sure. I don't know anything about the digestion of sloths."

"Well, someone needs to take point on sloth

digestion so we don't miss these in the future," Harry says as he writes down our answer.

It's Monday night, which is trivia night for our team, The Smartinis. I haven't made it to many trivia nights since I started working for Carter, so Harry's friend Carla has been filling in for me. Tonight, though, it's the OGs. I've been down in the dumps, and I hope a night out with my closest friends will help.

It's been a little over a week since I saw Carter for more than five minutes. When he gets home, I either have one of my friends there, or I try to slip out one door when he's coming in another one.

I had to stay to talk to him about Charlotte's math grade today, but I left as soon as the conversation was over, even though he asked me to stay.

I've avoided him for too long. We have to talk at some point, but the more I try to sort out my feelings for him, the more confused I get.

It's not that I'm not in love with him—I am. I didn't mean for it to happen, but I feel for him anyway. He's everything I've never had and didn't know I wanted. Devoted to his nieces, who are like his own daughters, earnest, honest and funny in his own way. Beneath his gruff exterior is a side of him the world doesn't get to see. It's that secret, soft underbelly that I love the most, but I even love the scowls.

He doesn't have the patience to sit through the halftime show when he's watching a football game, but he watches Pixar movies with us and never complains. No matter how tired he is, he reads to Hallie for at least thirty minutes at bedtime every night. Once he figured out how much I love Nutter Butters, he started buying them in bulk.

I don't know why I can admit to myself that I'm in love with him, but I can't admit it to him. When he got vulnerable and said he wanted us to be together for real, I panicked. Since we've only known each other for three months and we've only very recently gotten romantically involved, it seemed too fast.

My gut told me it takes years to build a deep, everlasting love and that a man who can fall in love this quickly can fall out of love just as fast.

But I miss him. I miss our phone calls after his road games. I miss hearing Hallie giggle from her bedroom when Carter's reading to her. I miss Olivia rolling her eyes when Carter tells her she's not allowed to talk to boys. I miss the way he looked at me during sex and the way he held me after.

"Suki?" Dex snaps his fingers in front of my face. "What animal never sleeps?"

"Oh. Uh...owls?"

"I'm telling you, it's bullfrogs," Mara says.

"Go with that," I say. "Mine was a total guess."

Harry gives me a sympathetic look. "Love on the brain?"

"Something like that."

"You two are driving me fucking crazy," Dex snaps.

Harry furrows his brow, confused. "Who two? Us two?"

"No, Suki and Carter. He's all, 'Grr, how's Suki? She won't talk to me,' and she's all, 'I love him, but I'm ignoring him.' Every time I'm over there with the kids and Carter gets home, I feel like a damn referee."

"So sorry to impose on you," I say, annoyed.

"Just own your shit. He's hurt because he said he loves you and you said you *probably* love him, too. Come on now, who isn't hurt by that? The only worse thing you could have said was *thank you*."

"He caught me off guard," I say defensively.

"So the best way to handle that is to kick him out and ignore him?"

"Who asked you?"

He laughs. "Babe, you should know by now that I don't need to be asked for my opinion to give it. He's kind of a caveman sometimes, but I'd kill for a man like that. Maim. I mean, can we trade lives for five minutes? So I can know what it feels like for your biggest problem to be that a crazy hot, rich pro athlete with a huge dick who buys you sweet presents is in love with you."

Someone clears their throat and we all look over at our server, who looks sheepish. "Just checking in. Drinks?"

"Another martini, please," Dex says.

"I'll take another glass of wine," Mara says.

"I'm good," Harry says.

"Me too."

We all return our attention to the trivia host.

"How many faces does a dodecahedron have?" he asks.

"Hmm. Dec means ten, right?" Harry says.

Harry is already writing. "It's twelve. It has a Greek root—it's a 3D shape with twelve pentagonal faces."

"Okay, but how often do you get to use the word pentagonal?" Mara says with a grin.

She's on cloud nine after having drinks with Professor Lumberjack. It went well—very well. I'm happy for her. She hasn't been excited about a man in a long time, and she's never had a relationship that lasted longer than a month. Maybe her time has come.

"I just don't want to get burned again," I say, returning to our conversation.

Dex puts his hand over mine and squeezes it. "I know. But real love is hot, babe. If it doesn't have the potential to burn you, it's not it."

I nod, thinking about what he said. It hits a nerve. Are my feelings for Carter terrifying because of how high the stakes are?

I've never lived with a man before him. Never had a man buy me a diamond. Hell, not even a cubic zirconia. I've never loved children or known how it feels to hurt when they hurt. No one's even done anything like the Nutter Butters for me other than my friends and family.

It's like I fell from a cliff when Tyler left, and then I swam to the shore and started climbing again. I climbed past that first cliff and kept going. And going. I climbed until I reached the highest point, and now I'm standing there.

If this relationship doesn't work out, I'll fall further. Harder. Even after a couple of months, Carter has set a much higher standard for men than I've ever known. He's not afraid to say he loves me, even if I don't say it back. He had a chance to let the girls' father raise them, but instead, he fought to keep them.

He's ten times the man Tyler was. And if he's willing to be vulnerable, I have to be, too.

I take a deep breath, returning my attention to the trivia host.

"Okay, guys. Bonus question here. This one is worth three points if you get it right. Here we go...the planet Uranus was originally named what?"

After a pause, he repeats the question. I look at Mara, then Dex, then Harry. All of them look as stumped as I am.

"Anyone?" Dex asks.

Mara shrugs. "My anus? That's all I've got."

He grins and starts writing. "We're going with it. My...anus."

"You guys," I say.

All three of them look at me.

"I know I'm a dumbass sometimes, but I'm a genius when it comes to picking friends. I love you so much."

Harry puts an arm around my shoulders and kisses my temple. "We love you, too."

Mara blows me a kiss.

Dex looks at me over the dark rim of his glasses. "I love you, Suki, which is why I'm telling you you'll regret it forever if you don't try with Carter. With your whole heart."

"Even though my heart looks like one of those

models of a smoker's lungs they show kids to scare them? All dark and shriveled?"

He considers. "Maybe you're right. If you end up an old spinster with nine cats, my nine cats will have someone to play with."

I roll my eyes. "I'll talk to him."

"Send him a tit pic," Mara says. "He won't even remember he was mad at you."

"Tit pics are your solution to every problem."

She shrugs. "They're not *not* a solution."

"How many tit pics have you sent to Professor Lumberjack?" Dex asks her.

"None."

"Oh." Harry's brows hit his hairline. "She really likes him."

The trivia host comes around to collect our answer sheets, and I take my phone out to check it.

Olivia: I got an A on my speech! I'll show you my teacher's score sheet tomorrow.

I get a pang of missing her, even though I just saw her this afternoon.

Carter and the girls have become everything to me. I've only ever asked myself what it would be like if things with Carter didn't work out. It's time to consider what things would be like if they did.

CHAPTER TWENTY-TWO

Carter

CHARLOTTE FROWNS at her plate and sets her fork down.

"What?" I ask.

"Nothing."

"What's the problem? Eat your breakfast. We have to leave for school in ten minutes."

Hallie carries her plate of French toast over to the trash can and dumps it.

"What are you doing? You just threw away your breakfast."

"I don't like it. I like it when Suki makes it."

I press my lips together for a few seconds to avoid snapping. You would think kids wouldn't be that picky about something as basic as French toast, but you'd be wrong.

"You guys drown it in syrup anyway. How can it taste that different?"

Charlotte cuts off another bite and eats it, her forlorn expression making it look like she's being force-fed prison gruel.

"Just find something to eat and be ready to go in"--I look at my watch--"eight minutes."

Olivia runs into the kitchen, her hair wet and her eyes wide with panic. "My hair dryer stopped working."

"What if I told you your hair will still dry? It'll just take longer."

"It'll dry frizzy, though! I can't go to school with frizzy hair."

I shrug, finishing the last lunch container of mandarin oranges, nuts and dried cherries for Charlotte's lunch. "Can you borrow Charlotte's dryer?"

Charlotte snort-laughs as she walks out of the pantry holding a half-eaten Twinkie. "I'm not high maintenance. I don't own a hair dryer."

"Can I borrow Suki's?" Olivia pleads.

"Yeah, I'm sure she won't care, but you only have six more minutes until I leave you behind and you miss school."

She sighs dramatically and races back upstairs.

FIFTEEN MINUTES LATER, I'm glaring out my windshield, my car idling in the driveway while I wait for Olivia.

"I don't want to be late for school," Charlotte grumbles from the back seat.

"Leave her here," Hallie says.

"How does Suki get you guys out of here at exactly seven forty every morning?"

"She doesn't sit on the toilet as long as you," Charlotte says.

I fight back a smile because that's completely true. But I've been starting my day with fifteen minutes of toilet time for more than a decade; I'm not changing.

Olivia runs out to the car, her expression frantic.

"Sorry," she says as she gets in, her hair dry and a giant Stanley cup in hand.

I turn on Taylor Swift and start the drive to school, glad today is just a practice day and I don't have to be at the arena until nine thirty.

"Uncle Carter, when is Suki coming back all the time?" Hallie asks.

I glance at her in the rearview mirror. "Hopefully soon."

"Why doesn't she want to see you?"

It's a punch in the gut to hear it put that way. "We just needed a break from each other, Hals."

"Just apologize for whatever you did," Charlotte says.

I balk. "How do you know it was my fault?"

"Who cares whose fault it was?"

I don't have a comeback for that. We listen to Taylor singing "I Can Do It With a Broken Heart" for around thirty seconds without talking.

"You could buy her a Taylor Swift shirt," Hallie suggests.

Her sweetness makes me smile. If only it were that easy.

"Maybe I should."

"Or you could get her a new plant. I saw one on my iPad that she doesn't have. It's called you licked a puss."

"What?" My jaw drops.

"Hallie!" Olivia scolds.

"What? That's what it's called. You licked a puss."

I burst out laughing, realizing how much I needed a moment of levity. "It's eucalyptus, Hals."

"Oh."

"Oh my God, Hallie," Charlotte says.

"Leave her alone. It's a big word and it's hard to pronounce."

I pull up to Charlotte and Olivia's school first.

"Make sure you've got your lunches and laptops and water bottles," I say. "If I have to come back and bring you anything, I'm coming to your classroom to give it to you in front of everyone and I'll kiss you on the cheek when I do it."

"I'd rather die," Olivia mumbles.

They get out of the car, Charlotte giving me a little wave on her way into school. I wave back and put the car into drive, heading out of the parking lot toward Hallie's school.

"I miss Suki," she says softly.

"Me too. I'm going to see her after practice and I'm gonna try to get her to come back."

She brightens. "Tell her I miss her. And don't say anything that will make her mad."

Wise words. I have to find a way to undo the damage I did by telling her I love her, which is ironic as fuck.

"Don't forget to give Darling treats today," Hallie says as I pull up to the drop-off door of her school.

"Uh-huh," I say wryly. "He might waste away." I wait for her to get out of the car. "Have a good day, Hals."

"You too."

On the drive home, I start to game plan what I'll say to Suki this afternoon. I plan to open by telling her how amazing she is and then swallow my pride and say I moved too fast.

I didn't. I was honest with her about my feelings, but if I have to lie and say I shouldn't have said it to get her back, I will.

We still have more than nine months left in our agreement, though I guess she could just decide the two hundred thousand dollars I already gave her is enough and bail. If she stays, she'll have a full year to decide whether I'm the guy for her.

If she's too jaded over Tyler to risk being hurt again, I'll have to accept that. It'll be really damn hard-- for me and the girls--but I can't force it.

Strong-arming my way into things works on the ice. It's actually often the only thing that works. But it won't help me with Suki. I have to let go and leave it in her hands.

Easier said than done.

———

WHEN I PULL onto my street a few minutes later, Sukis car is parked in the driveway. My pulse hammers in my ears and I speed up. When I get into the garage, I throw the car into park and run into the house.

Suki's sitting on the kitchen floor with Darling,

scratching his ears. He's nuzzling against her, totally content.

"Hey," she says softly.

"Hey." I set my keys down on the counter. "How are you?"

"I'm okay."

I tamp down a flare of aggravation. She's okay? I'm sure as hell not.

What if she's here to pack her things and leave? The thought makes me feel physically sick.

"Listen, I was in the wrong the other day," I say. "I called you broken, and that's so far from what I really think. I'm sorry."

She gets to her feet, Darling snorting for more attention. She walks over to the sink to wash her hands.

"You weren't wrong. You said you shouldn't have to fix what Tyler broke, and that's true."

Fuck. She's about to leave me; I can feel it in her tone.

"I want to, though," I say. "I can't take back what I said about loving you--because I do. But if you're not there yet, that's okay. I shouldn't have jumped you like that."

She turns to look at me, and I can't read the emotion in her eyes.

"If not for the girls, you never would have

noticed me. Like, if we'd met under different circumstances."

This hurts. It's an ache in my chest. But my hockey instincts won't work with her. I can't fight just for the sake of fighting.

"You're right. I wouldn't have noticed you. And I would have missed out on the most incredible woman in the entire world."

Her expression softens. I resist the urge to walk over to her and try to pull her into my arms.

"Suki, the girls are like daughters to me now, and they will be forever. We'll never forget Rachel, but we also have to move on. And I'm their parent now. How many men get a chance to see how a woman parents his children from the day they meet? How many men get to see a woman heal their children?"

Tears fill her eyes. "It wasn't just me, Carter."

"It was more you than anyone. And even though it probably means I'll lose you, I have to be honest. Yeah, the way you feel about the girls and the way they feel about you is part of the reason I love you. But I also love you in every other way a man should. You're smart, funny, sexy and...everything. You're everything and more. I come home to you because I want to. I don't want other women because I look at you and..." I clear the emotion from my throat. "How could I?"

She looks away, tears falling from her eyes to her cheeks. "We didn't start in a traditional way, and I'm carrying baggage that makes it hard for me to just fall in love."

I nod, her words a knife to my heart.

"But I did anyway," she says through tears. "I do love you, Carter. I don't know when it happened and it's really scary, but...I love you. And you know I love the girls."

Our eyes lock and I'm pulled toward her. I put my hands on her upper arms, then drop to my knees in front of her.

"Suki, I know it's fast. And we can wait if you want to. I'll prove whatever you need me to. But..." I take a breath, fighting a lump in my throat. "I'm in love with you, and all I want in this world is for you to stay married to me forever. Or marry me again, I don't know. Whatever you're willing to give me, I want it."

She's radiant as she smiles and cups my face in her hands. "Yes. You and the girls are my life now."

I lean forward, unable to keep a couple tears from falling as I lean my forehead against her stomach. She smooths a hand down my hair and then bends down, getting on her knees, too.

Putting my hands on her hips, I kiss her, tasting

the salt of our tears. Then I kiss her again, happiness and relief making me feel weak.

Darling comes over, snorting and nudging Suki's hand with his snout. She smiles at me.

"Our son wants some attention."

I groan and laugh. "Are you fucking serious?"

"He's part of the family."

I don't know if Hallie got it from Suki or vice versa, but Hallie's always saying that.

"Fuck it." I rub the top of his head. "Darling, you're uglier than I thought my son would be, but looks aren't everything, right?"

"Stop it, he's adorable."

"Maybe our future kids will look more like you. I hope so, anyway."

Our eyes meet, anticipation building inside me as I wait for her response.

"I wouldn't mind a serious little boy with dark hair like yours."

I wrap my arms around her and kiss her again, more passionately this time.

"I'm gonna have to miss practice today," I murmur against her lips.

"Are you sure?"

"Yep. My wife's talking about babies, I've got work to do."

She arches a brow. "Work, huh?"

"That's right. And I'm a model employee." I kiss her cheek, then the side of her neck. "I'm very dedicated to my work. Kind of a workaholic, actually." I squeeze her ass and she gasps with surprise. "I've got a home office in our bedroom, want to see it?"

She grins. "Absolutely."

CHAPTER TWENTY-THREE

Suki

SIX MONTHS LATER

"What are you wearing, Mrs. Stanton?" Carter wraps his arms around my waist from behind and I lean back into him, smiling. "I'm not sure I want other men seeing this much of my wife."

He nuzzles my jawline, a couple days' worth of beard growth sending a little shiver through my body.

We're at the very private Hawaiian vacation home of Carter's team owner, billionaire Hudson McClain. It's paradise—a tropical compound with nine bedrooms, twelve bathrooms and two pools. Carter and I renewed our vows on the beach at sunset two days ago with all our family and many friends in attendance. This afternoon, we're alone on the balcony of our suite, which has a sweeping view of the ocean.

"What, this?" I tease, turning to face him. "Just wait 'til you see the dress I'm wearing to dinner tonight."

Having a husband who openly lusts after my body has built my confidence up a lot. Today I'm wearing a black bikini with a Hawaiian print wrap skirt that has a slit all the way up the side of one thigh.

"Yes, that, you vixen." He tugs on my ponytail. "You want to be my wife; you better put a shirt on. You're dressed like you want to be my whore."

"Maybe I want both."

He kisses me, squeezing my ass. His erection presses against me and I murmur a laugh into his mouth.

"Apparently twice this morning wasn't enough for you?"

He hums and dips his head to kiss one of my full breasts. "I see these and all I can think about is you riding me the other night while they bounced in my face."

I groan, my body reacting to his mouth on my skin. "I wish we could do an encore right now, but we're supposed to be downstairs in two minutes to leave."

"They'll all understand why the newlyweds are late."

"Yeah, probably. Including my dad."

That sobers him right up. He moves back with a grunt.

"I don't get him. He sleeps with his wife, right? Why does he expect me not to sleep with you?"

I put a palm on his chest. "Because I'm his daughter. And it's not that he expects that; he just doesn't want it thrown in his face. If we show up late and my hair is a mess and my cheeks are flushed, that's kind of a dead giveaway. And you guys are just starting to get along."

Carter laughs and runs a hand through his hair. "So him not trying to fight me anymore is us getting along?"

It was only one time, but it did happen. Carter and I went to visit my parents a few months ago for their anniversary party. My dad had too much to drink and got all puffed up in front of his brother and friends. It took my brothers taking him aside and telling him Carter could a hundred-percent kick his ass to make him finally back down.

"He got to walk me down the aisle and he's happy about that."

Carter nods. "Hopefully that was enough for him to not stab me and toss my body overboard when we go fishing tomorrow."

I give him a look. "You'll be fine. Let's get down there."

When I turn to walk back inside, he smacks my ass. "Seriously, though, put on a shirt. I don't want to be hard in front of your parents."

I smirk playfully. "Seriously, no. That sounds like a *you* problem."

———

"Do you like it?" Charlotte smiles as she shows me the vase she made at the little pottery studio we're at.

"I love it."

"It's kind of ugly."

I lower my brows. "No, it's not. It's very organic. It reminds me of an ocean wave."

"I could paint it blue."

"I think you should."

"Check mine out." Dex holds up a mask he made by pressing a slab of clay to his face.

"Oh, I should have done that!" Charlotte grumbles.

"Well, let's make you one, girl," he says. "I'll help."

My three closest friends have become family to

all of us. They're over for dinner all the time, and Harry is teaching Olivia how to cook. Carter even invited Dex and Harry to his bachelor party, which meant a lot to me.

Several of his teammates are here with us. Four of them and two non-hockey-player friends were his groomspeople. My bridespeople were my brothers, Dex, Harry and Mara. The girls were all junior bridesmaids.

Our wedding was perfect. This time, Carter and I wrote our own heartfelt vows. I slid his ring back onto his finger. Back home, I borrowed it for a few days and had it engraved with the words "At Last" because our song is "At Last" by Etta James.

He added a beautiful band to my existing ring, and I cried when I read the engraving, which says, "At Every Table, I'll Save You a Seat." His thoughtfulness in using one of my favorite Taylor Swift Lyrics melted me.

Carter is sitting at a table with some teammates, looking engrossed in a conversation with Bash. He catches my gaze and motions for me to come over.

When I get to their table, Carter wraps an arm around my waist, resting the side of his face against my side.

"She gives amazing advice," he says to his best friend. "Tell her about it."

Carter stands up, kisses me and walks away, going over to the table where Hallie and Mara are working on something.

"What's up?" I say, taking Carter's seat.

Bash looks miserable. He has dark circles under his eyes and the corners of his mouth are turned down. I thought he looked bad because he's been drinking so much more than usual here and he's hungover. There must be something else going on.

He sighs heavily. "Right before we left for this trip, I found out an old friend got engaged. It's the younger sister of my best friend growing up, her name's Lainey. And she's marrying this absolute douchebag." He shakes his head. "It makes me sick."

"Do you and her have a history together?"

He looks away. "Not really. She made a move on me once, but I put her in the friend zone because she's Eric's sister."

"So this is just brotherly concern on your part?"

"Yeah, I mean...I care about her. I don't want her making the biggest mistake of her life."

"What does her brother think about the guy she's marrying?"

"Eric?" He scoffs. "He doesn't get it. He says Shane's changed from when I knew him in high school and he's great for Lainey."

"But you don't think so?"

"Hell no." He shifts in his seat, looking like he wants to go run some sprints or something to burn off extra energy. "Lainey's only twenty-four, she doesn't need to be getting married yet."

"How often do you see her?"

He shrugs. "I go home in my offseason and for holidays. A few times a year, my brother and a big group of friends from home come to my games and she'll be there."

Carter returns, setting a piña colada with a little pink umbrella in it in front of me and a bottled Corona in front of Bash. I look up and smile at him.

"Do you feel like you can be honest with Lainey about what you think of Shane?" I ask.

He balks. "She won't listen. That girl's so stubborn I couldn't even convince her the sky's blue. She's got a temper, too."

I sip my drink, thinking. There are no easy answers for this one.

"I'm not sure there's much you can do," I say. "But if it were me, and I cared about her, I'd still try. I'd have a private, in-person conversation where I shared the things her fiancé has done in the past few years that you're concerned about."

He takes a long pull on his beer. "There is nothing from the past few years. It was all stuff in high school."

"Oh."

"He's a fucking asshole and she'll be so unhappy with him. He'll want to get her knocked up right away with a little receding-hairline Shane Jr., and then she'll really be stuck." He shakes his head and takes another drink. "Fuck it. Might as well just drink 'til I don't care anymore."

Bash is very agitated. I meet Carter's gaze and see concern there. I know what's going on, but I'm not sure he does.

"So...do you think it's possible that maybe...you might have some feelings for Lainey?" I say.

"Me? Fuck no. No way. That's insane. I just don't want to see her stuck with that douchebag for the rest of her life."

"Right." I clear my throat. "I think you should talk to her as soon as you can. In person."

"Yeah, maybe. Someone has to talk some sense into her."

Carter goes over to him and claps him on the back. "You want to go to the bar and grill next door and get something to eat?"

Bash shakes his head, then finishes his beer. "This group activity thing is a cool idea, but I don't feel like being around anyone right now. I think I'm gonna go back to my room and take a nap."

"Okay, man. Let me know if you need anything," Carter says.

Bash looks at me and says, "Thanks, Suki. It feels better just to talk it over with you."

"You don't have to do anything here you don't feel like doing. We get it. Just take care of yourself, okay?"

He nods. "Thanks. I'll be at the luau thing tonight."

Looking like a dejected puppy, he walks away. Carter puts his arm around my waist.

"I'm worried about him," he says. "This doesn't seem like something he should be so worked up over."

I wrap my arms around him. "The issue is that he's in love with her, babe."

Carter gives me a befuddled look. "No, he's not. You heard what he said."

"I also read his tone and saw his expression and heard his irrational reasoning for being against the marriage."

Brow furrowed, my husband seems to be considering. "Maybe you're right."

"I'm right."

"He better get his ass to his hometown and see what he can do about it."

"He at least needs to talk to her."

"Yeah." He kisses my forehead. "Do you know how happy I am that I never have to deal with that shit ever again?"

I laugh. "What, love shit? I'm sorry to break this news to you, but you will still have to deal with love shit even though we're married."

"No, I mean single-people shit. I've got my girl and that's all I'll ever need."

My stomach flips over the sweetness of his words. I stretch up on my toes to kiss him. "You keep playing your cards right and we'll have to go back to our room for some married-people shit."

He grins. "I love married-people shit."

UP NEXT

The second book in the Love on the Line series is
Wanting the Winger.

ACKNOWLEDGMENTS

Even though I'm not a super people-y person, I went to the fall 2024 RAM conference, because Skye Warren puts it on and it's fabulous. My metaphorical cup got unexpectedly filled at that event. Presentations by Melanie Harlow and Piper Rayne reinvigorated me in so many ways. One evening at the conference, I got out my computer to plan a new series, which is Love on the Line. I'm grateful to Skye, Melanie, Piper and so many other authors who give of their time and talents to help other authors.

My roommate at the conference, Genevieve Jack, is my ride or die in the author world. I hope I never have to do this job without her by my side. Chelle Bliss, Sara Whitney, Kate Bateman and Skye Malone are also dear author friends who help me through the hard parts of writing books. Love you guys.

My beta readers Christina Gamboa, Jess Hodge and Brittani Brown know me and roll with my unorthodox ways. This book is better because of you three. (Christina, this book is DONE because of you. Lol.)

My editing and proofing team of Rosa Sharon and Jackie Ziegler are such an important part of this book. I'm so grateful for them.

And readers, huge thanks to you! You keep me writing and it's a dream come true. I always envision a book in my head and hope I can bring it to the page like I see it. Sometimes it comes out just like I wanted it and other times it's more of a challenge. This book is one I'm very proud of. It just flowed and felt good, even though I still struggled to finish it on time.

I hope this book put a smile on your face. Getting in bed with a book I'm loving is a vibe for me that's high on my self-care list. My greatest hope when I release a book is that I can give that same feeling to my readers.

ABOUT THE AUTHOR

Brenda Rothert lives in Central Illinois with her husband, children and three dogs. She loves to hear from readers through her website or her Facebook Group, Rothert's Readers.